Baked With Love 2
The Boardwalk Bakery Romance

TINA MARTIN

BAKED WITH LOVE 2

Chapter 1

"WHY AREN'T YOU answering your phone, Gianna?" Ramsey asked the question as he sat in his Range in the parking lot of the building that housed Wedded Bliss. While still in Charlotte, he wanted to see Gianna before he drove back home to Lake Norman, but she wasn't answering her phone and he was growing more anxious. More worried. Why? Because she had *the* appointment with Gemma's doctor today that would determine if Gemma's first round of chemotherapy had worked. He wanted to know if it did or didn't. Hopefully, it did. Then he'd at least know she was on the path to beating this thing and if she came out a winner, then so would Gianna. But what if it hadn't worked?

He sighed heavily and tapped his thumbs on the steering wheel. Should he drive to her house and wait there? No. Gianna wouldn't like that. What about call every oncology doctor in Charlotte until he found the office where she'd taken Gemma? That was absurd, but he was giving it serious consideration. He had to find Gianna somehow.

He blew a breath, leaned forward and rested his forehead on the car's steering wheel. He could shut off the engine, get out of the car and go back to Felicity's office. She would know the name of Gemma's doctor. But he'd rattled Felicity's nerves so bad, she probably couldn't take much more of him today. He came at her pretty strong with his proposal – with his insistence that she do her best to get Gianna to sign the papers. He could see the smoke coming out of her ears now if he stepped a foot back into her office.

He sat up and reclined in his seat. Maybe Gianna just didn't want to talk right now. She was in big sister mode, taking care of Gemma. She needed to concentrate, right? Needed to focus. To pay attention to the doctor's every word so she would know how to properly take care of Gemma when they returned home. But he needed to know that everything was okay. He was so desperate, he even considered sending a text message. Everyone who knew Ramsey knew he abhorred texting. He'd rather read an email than a text. He was an in-your-face kinda guy, and if for some reason you couldn't be in his face, a phone call would suffice. But text messages? No way. But maybe texting was her thing – the way introverts preferred to communicate. He wondered if she would reply to a message if he'd sent one. Then again, if he sent her a message and she didn't reply, he'd feel even more anxious.

He was stuck, but while he was waiting in limbo, he decided to make the best use of his time. So, he turned up the air conditioning a little, pulled in a few breaths and pressed the phone button on the steering wheel and said, "Call Judy Keffer."

Ramsey listened to the phone ring, then heard Judy's voice. "Good afternoon, Mr. St. Claire."

"Judy, hi. How are you?"

"Good, Sir."

Her voice was clear and professional. That's what he liked about having Judy as his secretary. She was efficient and did her job the way he liked it done. But sometimes he didn't like the way she shied away from telling him certain things, like if an email needed to be answered immediately, or if she had to be out of the office for a few hours to deal with some personal issues.

"How is everything at the office?" he asked.

"It's going okay," she said. "I flagged you on a few key emails that need your immediate attention."

"Good. I'll check into those when I get home. Right now, I need you to do something for me."

"Of course, Sir."

Looking at the photos he'd taken of Gianna's bills on his phone, he said, "I need a good contact for a company called Queen City Properties, and by *good* contact, I mean the head person in charge."

"Sure, thing. I'll see what I can find. Do you want me to email it to you later today?"

"No. Actually, I need it right now."

"Oh," she said, sounding surprised. "O-kay, Mr. St. Claire. Just give me a moment. Would you like for me to place you on hold while I type?"

"No," Ramsey said, listening as her fingers worked the keyboard.

"Ah...here we go," Judy said. "The owner's name is Dustin Claiborne. His number is 704-555-2009."

"Can you repeat that?" he asked, taking a silver pen from his suit jacket. As she repeated the number, he scribbled it on the back of the most recent copy of *Architectural Digest* that he'd taken from the passenger seat.

"Perfect. Also, I need a number for Pinnacle Funding?"

Judy quickly looked it up, then called out that number as well.

"Thank you. I appreciate it, Judy."

"You're welcome, Sir. And—"

Ramsey was about to hang up when he heard her say *and*. "Was there anything further, Judy?"

"Yes. Actually, there is. I have a question."

"Okay. What is it?"

"You're off this month," she said.

"That's not a question, but yes, I am."

"And I'm your secretary."

"Judy, get to the point. What's your question?"

"I was wondering if—if I could work from home a few days a week until you're back. It would be nice to have some flexibility with the kids and—"

"You can work at home as much as you like, Judy, but if I have the slightest feeling that the quality of your work is diminished by your not being present in the office, I will ask you to work from the office."

"No worries, Sir. I'll stay on top of everything."

"See to it that you do. Now, is there anything else?"

"No, Sir."

"Alright. Enjoy the rest of your day."

"You do the same, Sir."

Ramsey ended the call then immediately dialed Dustin Claiborne of Queen City Properties.

"Queen City Properties. This is Dustin."

The man had the heaviest, countriest accent Ramsey had ever heard. It always baffled him how big city people – and Charlotte was a big city – had the accent of someone from a country backwoods town – town people have never heard of before like Colerain, North Carolina. "Good morning, Dustin. This is Ramsey St. Claire."

"Oh. What can I do for you, Mr. St. Claire?"

Ramsey could hear the recognition in the man's voice. While he was sure Dustin didn't know him personally, it was apparent to him that Dustin had heard of St. Claire Architects. Maybe he'd read about them. St. Claire

Architects was a big deal in Charlotte.

"I want to inquire about a property you've leased out at the Shoppes at University Place. The—"

"You mean out there at the boardwalk?" Dustin interrupted to ask.

"Yes. That area."

"I got a slew of properties out there. Which one are you interested in?"

If you would allow me to finish talking, I'd tell you. "The Boardwalk Bakery."

After a slight chuckle, Dustin responded, "Well, ain't that a co-inky-dinky? If you're interested in that space, it'll be up for grabs real soon, partner. I'm putting the owner out on her tush as soon as the thirty-first rolls around. She's late on the lease. Apparently, she ain't selling enough cupcakes." Dustin chuckled.

Ramsey's jaw hardened. It's a good thing he was talking to *country Dustin* over the phone because if this was a face-to-face meeting, he'd put hands on the man. Even now, he tried to let the comment roll off of his back and if the comment was made about him, he probably would have. But Dustin was talking about his *Cupcake* and he couldn't let that ride. "Any, what's so funny, man?"

"Oh, just a little humor. I didn't mean nothing by it."

"You're actually laughing at someone else's misfortune?"

"Whoa, Mr. St. Claire...I think we're getting off on the wrong foot here, buddy."

"I'm not your buddy and my feet are fine. It's

your feet that are crossing over into territory where it doesn't belong."

"My apologies, Sir. Sometimes I go off on a tangent. I get that way when tenants don't pay their rent on time."

Ramsey didn't want to give him a cent. Not one copper penny. But he knew how much Gianna liked this location and besides that, the boardwalk was prime real estate for businesses. So, swallowing his irritation, he asked, "When does the lease expire?"

"Well, it's supposed to expire at the end of the year, but I'm not sure if it'll go that far seeing as how the property is two months behind on the lease.

"Two months behind..." Ramsey repeated.

"Yes, Sir."

"Okay, here's what I want."

"Yes, Sir. I'm listening."

"I want to pay off the current balance and renew the contract for the next ten years."

"You say what now?"

Ramsey frowned so hard, his forehead tightened. "I said, I want to pay off the current balance and renew the contract for the next ten years."

The man chuckled. "I admire your ambition, Mr. St. Claire, but we only offer five-year leases. Not ten, and I'm sure you know why. In ten years, the lease could increase on a property by ten percent. Maybe even fifteen."

"Yeah, it could, but that's no guarantee."

"Well, I don't know if I'm willing to take that gamble. I'd be short changing myself if I locked this property in for ten years. Five years is all I can offer you."

"Maybe I didn't make myself clear," Ramsey said. "I want to lock in the lease for ten years. I'll pay you the $120,000 today, in addition to the past due amount of $2,100."

Dustin chuckled. "Ten years it is, then!"

That's what I thought. "Have the new lease dropped off at St. Claire Architects."

"Over there on IBM drive?"

"Yes. I won't be there, so ask for Regal St. Claire when you get to the receptionist's desk."

"Sounds good to me. I'll be there before five, Sir."

I bet you will. "And there's no need to notify the owner of the lease update. I've already taken care of that." Actually, he hadn't but he would.

"Alright, Mr. St. Claire. Nice doing business with you, Sir."

Whatever, moron. "Yep." Ramsey hung up the phone and immediately voice-called Regal.

"What's up, Ram?"

"Hey, FYI. Dustin Claiborne from Queen City Properties is going to stop by there today."

"Why?" Regal asked. The name didn't ring a bell.

"To pick up a check for $122,100."

"What business do we have with Queen City Properties?"

"*We* don't. I do. It's for Gianna's bakery."

"Whoa. You're investing in this chick now?"

Ramsey smiled. *If that's what you want to call it.* "I am. I need you to cut the check for me since I'm not coming over there today."

"No problem. I got it handled, but dang, Ram. You're going all-in for this girl, huh?"

"It's only money, Regal. It's not like it'll set me back any. Even if it did, I'd still do it. For her, anyway. She's worth it. She's worth a lot more."

"What's the latest with that Wedded Bliss situation? Did you talk to Gianna's friend yet? What's her name? Felicity, was it?"

"Yes, and I did talk to her but I didn't go your route of trying to juice her for information. I told her to convince Gianna to sign the marriage agreement."

"What!"

Ramsey grinned. He thought his brother would find that interesting. He didn't expect that he'd pop a blood vessel. "You want to marry her?"

"Yes. I want to marry her. It's the perfect arrangement, don't you think? You can't tell me that these individual happenings are coincidences. On a whim, I sign up for Wedded Bliss. Without even knowing why I walk into The Boardwalk Bakery. The owner of Wedded Bliss and the owner of The Boardwalk Bakery are best friends. These occurrences all came together for me and Gianna, and I was going to marry someone anyway. I had given up hope of meeting anyone who could actually mean something to me. Then she comes along..."

"I hear you man, but you're forgetting the reason you joined Wedded Bliss in the first place. You were looking for a woman who would fulfill the roles of a wife in your life, yet remain distant enough that you could never love her. Is that what Gianna is?"

Ramsey closed his eyes briefly. "I can't tell you what Gianna is right now."

"Then why do you want to marry her? I get it—you have this weird fascination with her, but you're taking it a step further with marriage, especially if you don't think you could fall in love with her. Be real with yourself, Ram. Does she have a chance? And ask yourself if you're willing to break her heart all because you need to fill a void."

"I know what I'm doing, Regal."

Regal sighed. For once, he doubted that statement. There's no way he would fall head over heels in love with Gianna when he'd been insistent that he would never fall in love again. Now, he was making plans to marry a woman whom he really didn't know and he knew what he was doing? "What if Gianna declines your request? What will you do then? Go back to Wedded Bliss and handpick some other woman?"

"No, I won't handpick another woman. I just have to make sure Gianna doesn't decline my offer. I'll talk more about it with you later. I have to make another call right now, Regal."

"Okay, Ram. I'll catch up with you later."

Ramsey pressed the button to end the call, thinking about what Regal had said. What if Gianna didn't go along with his plan? He told Felicity to lay out the details to her on Friday which meant he had all day today, Tuesday,

Wednesday and Thursday to make Gianna realize how much she needed him. He was fully aware of his need for her.

Chapter 2

On the way home from the doctor's office, Gemma looked at Gianna as she drove. Her eyes were hidden behind a pair of brown-tinted sunglasses. "Do you have enough money to get some soup from Panera, Gianna?"

Gianna glanced over at Gemma then returned her attention back to the road. She actually wanted to stop for lunch? That was a first. Lately, Gemma had been so sick, the only place she wanted to go was her bedroom. "I'm sure I can find ten dollars in my purse somewhere. Do you really feel up to eating out because I can always cook something when we get home?"

"No. Let's stop since we're already out," Gemma said. While she was still somewhat alert, she wanted to enjoy some time with her sister instead of going home and lying in bed for the rest of the day. She'd be too exhausted to do anything else and once her head hit that pillow, that was all she wrote. Even if she wasn't sleeping, it would be hard to get up. And she knew Gianna was tired, too. As it was, she had to get up at the butt-crack of dawn, get herself ready and then help her get ready. The last thing she wanted was for Gianna to get home, prepare lunch for her, then turn around and cook dinner, too. It was too much, and she hated that all the responsibility fell on Gianna.

* * *

SITTING AT A spacious booth in Panera Bread, waiting for someone to bring over the broccoli cheddar soup and French baguettes they'd both ordered, Gemma stared at her sister. Gianna had been suspiciously quiet since leaving the doctor's office and while she had an idea why she wanted to talk about it.

"Gianna?"

Gianna looked up at her pale sister, watching a happy expression come to her face. A pleasant smile. Sick and all, she could still manage a smile, and that made *her* smile "Yes, Gemma?"

"Talk. Why are you so quiet?"

"I don't know what to say." *Well, I do know what to say but I don't know how we're going to get you better. I don't know how I'm going to manage the bakery and take care of you. You need me more than anything right now and I can't take care of you because I'm working – working to take care of you financially but I want more than anything for you to be taken care of health wise and I'm failing you.*

"You don't know what to say about what the doctor..." Gemma coughed. "What doctor Willoughby said?"

"I don't understand it. I'm trying to process

it, but this nightmare just seems to keep getting worse." Gianna tried to stop herself from saying *that* much but it came out, anyway. She didn't like discussing her concerns with Gemma, especially since she always looked at Gemma as a child – her child – and she was the adult taking care of her. And as an adult, parents didn't offload their woes on their kids no matter how bad circumstances were. They sucked it up, held it all in and looked for ways to solve the problems while the kids went on to live their lives. That's what Gianna wanted to do. She wanted Gemma to be happy even though she was sick – an oxymoron she knew because how can you be happy when you're sick – but still, she wished happiness for her sister and she thought chemotherapy was a pathway to that happiness. But it failed. "How does chemo *not* work? That's the treatment for cancer and it didn't work. I don't get it."

Gemma cleared her throat. "Okay, so what? The chemo isn't working. It's not the end of the world."

Losing you would be the end of my world. Gianna took a sip of water to dispel the urge to cry.

"Besides, I got new pills now," Gemma said. "Maybe they will do what the chemo couldn't do."

Gianna inhaled a breath and briefly covered her face with her hands.

"Gianna, will you stop stressing out? Everything is going to be alright," Gemma told her.

Gianna forced a smile even though a tension headache throbbed at her temples. How was it that Gemma – the one suffering, the one battling cancer – more optimistic than she was? It was a testament to her strength – to the realization of knowing she had a disease that could possibly take her life but she still found a reason to be hopeful. To smile.

The soup arrived and Gemma inhaled a whiff of it. "Mmm...smells sooo good."

"It does." Gianna tasted hers. "It's hot, so be careful."

"Yes, mommy," Gemma teased.

Gianna smirked.

"Speaking of mommy, have you heard from ours lately?"

"Nope," Gianna said and left it at that. Talking about her mother would incense her and she wanted to enjoy this time – these memories – she was having with her sister. She never knew if it would be the last they'd make. "I can't believe I left my phone home."

"You didn't need it anyway, well unless you were waiting for a call from Ramsey." Gemma waggled her eyebrows.

Gianna hid a smile. "No, I wasn't waiting for a call from Ramsey."

"Yes, you were." Gemma laughed. "Look...you can't even talk about him without your cheeks turning red."

"Sure I can," Gianna said, manually pressing her cheeks to flatten them, thus ridding her face of the smile that was so prevalent whenever Ramsey was the subject. Then she said, "I *would* like to know what possessed him to spend the night without my approval."

Gemma twisted her mouth. "How could you approve anything while you were sleeping?"

"Okay. You have a point."

"Besides, he seems like a nice guy. I had a lil' chat with him last night after you fell asleep." Gemma dipped a piece of bread in the creamy, cheesy broccoli soup, then chewed it.

"You had a chat with him? Seriously?"

"Umm...hmm," she hummed. "And guess what, Gianna? I think he *really* likes you and I'm not talking friend-like. I'm talking smoochy-smoochaay." Gemma puckered her lips.

Gianna didn't know why she suddenly felt embarrassed but she did. She glanced around the immediate area where they were sitting then whispered across the table to Gemma, "Gem, put your lips down. He doesn't like me in that way."

Gemma laughed. "Why are you whispering? He's not in here. Or maybe he is, looking like that double fudge brownie I saw in the display case."

"Gem!" Gianna whispered loudly.

Gemma continued laughing. "Gianna, you've got to be out of your mind if you think that man doesn't have the hots for you."

Gianna's mouth turned up in the corner. "Men have the hots for Victoria Secret models—not flour-slanging cupcake girls. There's no way a man of his prestige would be attracted to plain, ol' me. No way."

"First of all, you're not old and you're not plain. You're as weird as they come, but not old and plain."

"Oh, that's reassuring. Thanks for reminding me of how weird and awkward I am, Gem."

Gemma cracked a smile. "You know what I mean."

"No, I don't. Care to explain, lil' girl?"

"Ugh...you need to loosen up and you really need to get out more. Goodness. Ramsey is attracted to you and it's because you're quirky. You're probably unlike any woman he's ever encountered and he finds that appealing."

Gianna's brows narrowed. "And you know this how?"

"I watch Lifetime and Hallmark all day, every day while I'm lying in bed. I've seen every romance movie that has ever been produced. Men don't want the same ol' same ol'. They want a woman who'll keep them on their toes. Keep them guessing. And God knows you have enough weirdness in your backpack to keep him guessing for the rest of his life."

Gianna couldn't help but giggle at the way her sister was cackling. "You can't compare real life to fictional TV movies."

"Yes, I can. You know why?"

"Why, Gem?"

"Because most movies are based on actual, real-life events."

"Not true."

"It is true."

"Okay. Fine. I'm not going to debate with you over movies, but what I will say is, if your theory is correct and Ramsey is interested in me because I'm a lil' different—"

"Not different. Weird," Gemma interrupted to clarify.

"Okay...weird, why is he the only man to ever want me?"

"He's not. I see the way men look at you. You just don't see it. Or maybe you do. You just refuse to acknowledge it, but I'm here to tell you...you're stunning."

Gianna lowered her cup to the table. "You're my sister. You *have* to say I'm stunning."

"But I mean it, Gianna. You're beautiful. You just don't apply yourself." *Because you're so busy taking care of me.*

"Well, thank you, Gem, but I doubt very seriously if Ramsey is interested in me like that." Maybe if she said it enough, she'd actually believed it, but honestly, she knew Ramsey liked her. Several times now, he'd smothered her with hugs. Even last night, sitting on the couch, he'd put his arms around her and she bathed in his scent. Felt comfort in knowing that he was there – so comfortable that she fell asleep. She'd never done that before – fallen asleep in a man's arms. She'd never let a man get that close. But with Ramsey, it was a different story.

"What if he is interested in you like that?" Gemma asked.

"He's not," Gianna said, dipping a piece of French bread into the soup.

Gemma cleared her throat. "Help me understand then. So, you don't feel anything when you're around him?"

Tickled, Gianna said, "*Feel* anything? Like what? What am I supposed to feel?"

"You know...chemistry. Tingly sensations. Vibes. Something along those lines."

"Yeah, I feel something...I feel nervous. He makes me nervous and jittery like I've had too much caffeine or something."

"Mmm, hmm. That counts as chemistry in my book."

Gianna smiled and shook her head, aimlessly stirring soup.

"What about when you look into his eyes?" Gemma asked.

"I can't look into his eyes—well, I—I can, but not for very long."

"Why not?" Gemma asked, tossing a soup-drenched piece of bread into her mouth.

"Because I feel like he's peering into my soul when he looks at me. It's freaky."

Gemma chuckled. "Oh, yeah. You like him."

Gianna blushed, then admitted, "Okay. I like him, a tad, but even if he was interested in me, which I *highly* doubt, I wouldn't know what to do with a man like Ramsey."

"You could fall in love with him."

"You say that like love is so easy."

"It can be. It's usually the people who make it difficult."

"Well, that's an insightful way of looking at it."

Gemma took another spoonful of soup into her mouth.

"On a more serious note, Dr. Willoughby

said you have to be very careful. With a weakened immune system, you can easily catch stuff, which is probably why we should've just gone home instead of stopping here."

"I'm alright, Gianna. Eat. I heard what the doctor said. I need to wash my hands frequently, use hand sanitizer, blah, blah, freakin' blah. Got it."

Gianna ate more of her soup and the two of them were quiet for a moment when Gemma asked, "What does he do?"

"Who? Ramsey?"

"Yeah."

"He's an architect."

"What about family? Does he have siblings?"

"Yep. His parents are still together and he has three brothers—Regal, Royal and Romulus."

"Cool."

"And they all work for St. Claire Architects," Gianna added.

"So, you and Ramsey *have* been getting personal, huh?"

"Ugh...will you quit it, Gem," Gianna said, smiling. Blushing.

Gemma tried to hold it in but she coughed again. This cough lasted longer than the others.

"Where is this coughing coming from all of a sudden? You weren't coughing like this during your check-up."

"I know. This soup probably just went down wrong. That's what I get for eating so fast but it's so good."

"Drink a little water," Gianna told her.

Gemma sipped water, then cleared her throat. "Ah...that's better."

"I think we should get going, anyway. It's almost your nap time."

"You make me sound like a defenseless infant."

"Well, you are my *baby* sister. I have to take care of you." *And I will take care of you, even if it kills me.*

* * *

When they arrived home, Gianna reminded Gemma to wash her face and her hands. Then, after Gemma changed into her pajamas, she helped her get comfortable in bed for an afternoon nap.

"The day is still young, Gianna. What are you going to do while I'm lying here being all lazy, watching movies?"

"I'll find something to do. Trust me."

Gemma yawned. "Just enjoy being off work today. Tomorrow, you'll be back on your feet again."

"Don't remind me," Gianna said. "Anyway, rest. I love you."

"Love you too, Gianna."

When Gianna closed the door to Gemma's bedroom, she was already in tears as she headed upstairs to her own bedroom. The doctor didn't give a good report on Gemma. The chemotherapy didn't work, and he prescribed her some pills just as a way of saying *there's nothing else we can do* without actually saying the words. If chemotherapy wasn't effective, what chance did Gemma have after a few measly pills?

In her bedroom, she sat on the bed, making herself breathe through the tightening of her chest. She wanted to scream. How else would she release this pain? Instead, she did what she did best – what she trained herself to do – internalize it all until it balled up inside of her so tightly, the pressure made tears come out of her eyes until they soaked her pillow. The pain, sorrow, the hurt would only subside when she was asleep.

Chapter 3

RAMSEY HAD TRIED getting in touch with Gianna a few more times after leaving the parking lot of Felicity's office. Still, she didn't answer, and it plagued him as to why she wasn't picking up. Was Gemma still at the appointment? Hospitalized? What was going on? Maybe it wasn't his business to know, but he didn't care if it was his business or not. He needed to know, and soon.

Deciding to go home and work off his frustration, he slid on a pair of gym shorts and a T-shirt and ran for thirty minutes nonstop on a tread climber. Then he did a round of pushups – a hundred straight – and chin lifts, too many to count. He was about to do some weight lifting when his phone rang. He pulled the soaked, T-shirt over his head, tossing it over to the wicker hamper, then walked over to the counter where his phone was. Hoping to see the caller was Gianna, he grew crestfallen when he realized it was his brother, Royal.

He answered, "Didn't Regal tell you I was off this month?" He wasn't close with Royal or Romulus for that matter, but Royal especially. And they rarely talked outside of work.

"He told me," Royal acknowledged, "But I

didn't believe him and my instincts were right since you were at the university site this morning, threatening McFarlane."

"*Threatening* is a strong word, Royal. You can come up with something better than that, can't you?"

"No. Threatening is spot on. That's what you do. Threaten people. You don't—"

"I *don't* make threats. I make promises. Now, I laid down my expectations for McFarlane and that's what I meant. If they're one day over the contractually agreed upon date, the late fees will apply."

"Two thousand dollars a day?" Royal said, sounding pissed.

"Yes. Two grand, and no, I don't care that you have a problem with it, Royal."

"I'm sure you don't. You don't care about anything but your massive ego."

He'd struck a nerve. *Ego?* As it was, Ramsey didn't want to talk work at the moment. He wanted to know where Gianna was, but instead, he had to listen to his *younger* brother rant about *his* ego? Seriously? "What does my ego have to do with these companies failing to honor their commitments? I'm done dealing with people, companies and corporations who don't do what they say they're going to do. As of late, most of these contractors we hire never hit their target dates. Going forward, if a contractor gives me a date, then I expect for the work to be completed, on or by *that* date. No exceptions. I don't care if they have to work overtime or hire more people as long as it gets done on the date they've contractually agreed upon. You should've known that this has been a recurring problem."

"Yes, I know it's a problem. That's why I'm getting a team together to work on it now. *I'm* the troubleshooter, remember?"

More like the troublemaker. "Right. You *are* the troubleshooter. So, should I blame you for the University City project running behind schedule?"

"If you feel like it, but pointing blame isn't going to make us operate any more efficiently, Ram. We need solutions."

Ramsey's brows snapped together when he said, "Then come up with some solutions, Royal."

"What do you think I've been doing?" Royal replied.

Ramsey shrugged. "Beats me. Every time I blink, you're taking time off. If you want this job, I do expect you to do some real work."

Royal hissed his displeasure in the form of a long sigh. "You're unbelievable."

"No. I'm real, and you can't handle the truth. You're used to everything being handed to you on a platter, but let me be the first to tell you— if you want this job, do it!"

"You know what...I'm going to get off the line. I don't know what crawled up your butt but call me back after you've had your fix...whatever that is."

Ramsey listened to the dial tone and placed the phone back on the shelf. He took a towel from the counter, wiped sweat from his face and walked to the kitchen to get a tall bottle of Voss water. Then he grabbed a green apple from the fruit bowl on the island, almost demolishing it in five bites. He tried calling Gianna again. But there was no answer from his *fix*.

* * *

AFTER TAKING A shower, Ramsey decided that enough was enough. He was done wondering. He decided to go see for himself how Gemma was doing and why Gianna wasn't answering her phone. When he pulled up in her driveway, he noticed her car was there. Gemma's appointment was early this morning. Right now, it was after five. The appointment had been long over. What had she been doing since then? Chilling at home, ignoring his calls?"

He rang the doorbell and waited...not hearing a sound. There was no creaking of the floor or the faint sound of a TV or radio playing. Nothing. Just silence. He pushed the doorbell again, frowning this time. "Where are you, Gianna?" he asked evenly. He pushed the doorbell again, twice more, and when he heard someone at the door, his anxiety lessened. He watched the door open slowly to reveal Gemma standing there with a beige scarf on her head. Her arms were crossed like she was cold.

"Hey, Ramsey," Gemma said softly.

"Hi, Gemma. May I come in?" he asked, taking a step forward before she could answer.

"Yeah. You can come in." She unlatched the lock that secured the storm door and he opened it.

When he stepped inside, he embraced Gemma while asking, "How did it go? What did the doctor say? Is everything okay?" He broke the hug to look at her when she replied.

"It was as I expected it would be. My doctor said chemo isn't working, so he started me..." Gemma coughed. "He's started me on some...some pills. And Gianna freaked out."

"What do you mean she freaked out?" he asked, his chest rising in and out quickly. The thought of something bothering Gianna bothered him, too. Made him feel a bout of panic. Where did that come from?

"She got quiet on me," Gemma explained. "That's what she does when she's upset and worried. Goes stone silent, and I know she cried herself to sleep. I just know it."

"Where is she?" he asked, his eyes scanning the living room, gazing on into the kitchen, looking for her.

"She went upstairs and hasn't been back down since."

"What time did you get home from the appointment?"

Gemma shrugged. "Two, something. Well, we left the appointment earlier than that. We stopped off for lunch at Panera Bread. What time is it now?"

Ramsey glanced at his watch. "It's 5:17 p.m. So, you're telling me she's been sleeping for close to three hours?"

"Um, yeah?" she said in the form of a question since she was uncertain if it was the answer Ramsey wanted to hear. "I could be wrong. Maybe she's watching TV or something. I don't know. What I *do* know is, I've been up for an hour and I haven't heard a peep from upstairs. I can usually hear her when she walks to the bathroom."

"Do you mind if I go up?" Ramsey asked.

"No. Not at all."

"Okay. Thank you," Ramsey said getting a head start, jogging up the beige carpeted staircase, traveling the hallway toward her room. Her bedroom door was closed. He turned the knob glad to find it unlocked. If it was locked, he'd probably use a shoulder thrust to knock it off the hinges. That's how badly he needed to see her.

Twisting the knob, he opened the door slowly. He saw her lying on the bed with her back toward him. His eyes traveled the silhouette of her clothed frame. He walked around the foot of her princess bed to see her face. Her eyes were closed. Breathing slow, yet steady.

He kneeled beside the bed and stared. According to Gemma, she'd been up here for three hours. That didn't mean she was sleeping for a full three hours though. He saw the remote on her nightstand. Maybe she'd watched TV. Or taken a shower. No, she was fully clothed. She hadn't showered. Maybe she was lying here, crying her eyes out after receiving the devastating news from the doctor.

That was more likely.

Ramsey opened the blinds hoping the subtle evening light would help her wake up naturally, then eased up on the bed and laid next to her. Faced her. He wanted to touch her, but since he'd rather she wake up on her own, he'd have to settle for the feel of her body heat blending with his and even that did something to rouse him. He closed his eyes. Absorbed it. Her heat. Her energy. Then he looked at her again, his eyes recording every detail of her face – the shape of her brows, the long eyelashes over those beautiful eyes he longed to see, her cutesy nose that he'd wiped flour from and lips that made his mouth water.

Watching her sleep was beginning to be one of his favorite activities. Even after fussing at some contractors, arguing with Royal and stressing out about Gianna's whereabouts, this moment – watching her sleep – took the cares of the day away. Made him forget problems. Made him want to glide the tip of his index finger along the shape of her lips. Just as the desire turned into a need, her eyes opened.

Gianna batted her eyes, focusing, then closed them again. She was dreaming about Ramsey. Again. How did she let him creep into her subconscious mind? It was bad enough she couldn't handle his presence in *real* life. Now, she had to be all anxious and jittery in her sleep, too? How was that fair?

She opened her eyes again – at least she thought she opened them – but if they were open, why was she still seeing his face? Weird.

Was she having one of those dreams where you're actually dreaming and you wake up but you only *dreamed* you woke up? Her forehead creased. She extended her hand to the vision of Ramsey's face and traced his lips. "Wow. They feel so real and warm," she said softly.

"That's because they *are* real. And warm." Ramsey smiled.

"Aaah!" Gianna screamed hysterically and sprang up off of the bed and right to her feet like a cat dodging a puddle. In full panic mode – Gianna-style – she patted herself down to make sure she was covered in clothes.

"Well, that wasn't the reaction I was expecting," Ramsey said, amused when he knew he shouldn't be. She actually looked terrified.

"What are you doing here? In my...in my bedroom?" she asked taking short breaths, looking at him like he was a stranger.

"I came to check on you," he said casually. Standing up on the opposite side of the bed from where she was standing, his tone grew serious when he asked, "Where's your phone, Gianna?"

Disoriented, Gianna asked, "My...my, my, my phone?"

"Yes," he said, sliding his hands into his pockets. "Your phone. Where is it?"

"It's...um...I don't know where it is," she said, unable to stop moving from side-to-side like she was looking for a good path to make a quick escape. Then, her eyes narrowed when she said, "For all I know, you took it."

He chuckled. "Why would I take your phone?"

"I don't know. *You* tell *me*."

A playful squint decorated his glowing eyes. "Okay, seriously, Gianna, where is your phone?"

"I *said*, I don't know."

"You don't know?" he said and began taking slow, easy steps towards her.

"Stay over there," she told him.

Ignoring her, he kept coming her way when he said, "I called you at least five times today, was worried so much I couldn't focus, and you don't know where your phone is? How can you *not* know where your phone is, sweetness?"

"My phone, my phone, my phone," she said hoping the repetition would jog her memory. "Where is my phone? Oh, that's right. I left it home." She rubbed her eyes, still waking up. "I was in a rush this morning and left my phone home," she explained to him. "It's probably in the kitchen somewhere. I'm not sure."

"Oh, yeah. That's right. We were in the kitchen last night before you fell asleep in my arms. On the sofa. In the living room," he said as if he wanted to remind her of that fact.

Gianna frowned as if his words didn't register. "Why are you here, Ramsey?"

"I'm here to check on you, and I wanted to know how Gemma's appointment went. I was concerned. I still am."

"It's nothing for you to be concerned about. Why are you here?" she asked again, her frown deepening this time.

"I just told you why I'm here. Are you not fully awake yet?"

"Yes! I'm awake, but I don't expect to wake up with a man in my bedroom."

"A *man*...you make it sound like we don't know each other...like I'm some dude off the street. You know me, Gianna."

"Not really, Ramsey. Look...I appreciate you being a listening ear for me last night. And I appreciate your offer to help me, but this whole thing of you being connected to me somehow is a little...um...how do I put this nicely? Out there? Yes, *out there*. And I don't know you well enough for you to be sneaking into my bedroom with your big hands and your...your freshly licked lips puckered up at me while I'm sleeping."

Smiling, Ramsey said, "They may have been freshly licked, but they definitely weren't puckered. I don't think men do that. Pucker."

"Well, whatever," Gianna said crossing her arms over her chest. "Your lips were doing something strange."

He narrowed his eyes. "My lips were doing something strange," he repeated slowly just so she could hear a playback of what she just said and how crazy it sounded. "And how do you know they were freshly licked?"

"Because they look glossy."

"Gianna—"

"Don't *Gianna* me. You can't go around climbing into people's bedroom windows and stuff, Ramsey."

He chuckled. "Okay, you're definitely not

awake."

"Why are you laughing at me?"

"Because you're hilarious."

Her eyes burned with annoyance. "And I'm *hilariously* about to call 911 on your fool behind."

Still laughing, Ramsey said, "Okay, call 'em, but you gotta..." He couldn't get the words out for laughing so hard. "You gotta find your phone first, sweetness."

"Go ahead. Laugh it up," she said, throwing a bath towel around herself like a cape since she wasn't in the right frame of mind to remember that her robe was hanging on the back of the bathroom door. And why did she even need a robe or a towel? She still had all her clothes on. It's not like she was wearing a flimsy nightgown. She was in a blouse and dark blue jeans. "Just wait 'til I find my phone. We gon' see if it's funny then. You're going to jail for breaking and entering."

Ramsey laughed so hard, he had to take his hands out of his pockets as he bent over to contain himself. "Okay...okay. Calm down, Gianna. Your sister...Gemma let me in. I didn't come through the window. Good grief. You are something else, woman."

"Whatever. And I don't want no breakfast, either. I just want to find my phone."

"Who said anything about breakfast?" he asked, still laughing. "It's actually dinner time."

She rolled her eyes, irritated by his laughter.

Ramsey continued chuckling, but she looked dead serious. That's what made her allegations so funny. Like he'd ever climb through anybody's window...

To determine if she was actually awake and not sleep-talking as he suspected, he asked, "Gianna, what's one plus two?"

"The number of years you're going to get for breaking and entering because I'm pressing charges."

"Woman, I did not break into your house."

"Then why are my blinds open?" she asked, looking up at him as he stood in front of her. "I *never* open my blinds."

"I opened them because I wanted the afternoon sunlight to wake you up. I didn't want to nudge you."

"Just go, Ramsey," Gianna said. "I'm still calling 911 when I find my phone."

Okay. Enough laughing. All humor dissipated when he realized she was serious. He didn't know if she was still sleeping or what, but he knew he had to take control of the situation. So, whipping out his phone, he handed it to her and said, "Here. Call 911. Tell them there's a man in your bedroom who doesn't want to do you any harm. Tell them he's here for you, to help you. To be a shoulder for you. To do anything you want him to. Call 'em."

She looked at the phone but didn't reach for it. "Ramsey..."

"No. Here. Call 911, Gianna."

She glanced at his phone again then back into his eyes. Briefly. "No. I don't want your phone."

"Then stop trying to make me go away because I'm not going anywhere. I'm not. I'm here to stay. Well, not permanently, but I told you...I'm here for you."

"How—why—what do you mean? You have a life. This—this is strange. *You're* strange."

"People who live in glass houses shouldn't throw stones, Gianna."

"I'll throw whatever the freak I wanna throw, *Ramsey*," she said, brightening her eyes at him.

He nibbled on his bottom lip, watching hints of green in her honeyed eyes – a sure sign that she was nervous. And the fact of the matter was, she looked delicious having just woken up and the way she pronounced his name...jeez. *Mmm, mmm, mmm.* He loved the delicate, sweet-sounding, Southern drawl she added to it. He'd never heard anyone say his name quite like her.

"What am I going to do with you?" he asked, touching her chin with his index finger and thumb.

"Leave me alone," she replied, ducking away from his touch.

"That's not going to happen," he told her.

"And you're just so sure of yourself, aren't you?" she asked, throwing a hand on her hip.

"I am. You definitely don't get to where I am in life by being *unsure* of yourself. So yes, I can say with confidence that I'm not going to leave you alone. I like you, Gianna Jacobsen, and one day, you'll like me just as much. Just think of me as your real-life guardian angel." He smiled, showing perfection.

She thought it was a sneaky smile but brilliant, nonetheless. *Gee, what am I thinking? Forget about his charming smile, Gianna. You have to get him out of here.* "Eight days ago, we didn't know each other."

He shrugged his large shoulders. "Now, we do. What do you want for dinner, Gianna?"

That's how she could get him to leave. She would send him out on a dinner run and not open the door when he returned.

"I'm not physically leaving in case you're thinking about locking me out," he said. Was he a mind reader, too? "I should be able to find something in the fridge to cook. Tell me what you want to eat."

And now, she lost the ability to speak. Was he serious? He certainly looked serious.

When she didn't respond, he said, "Okay. I'll just wing it. When you've finished waking up, join me downstairs."

* * *

THE KITCHEN WAS stocked pretty good since she'd just bought groceries the night before. Well, he had ended up paying for the groceries, and he followed her home to help her unpack them and put everything away. Surely he could find something to whip up for her. He opened the refrigerator door and surveyed the contents – eggs, milk, cheese, ham...

"I see you've made yourself right at home."

He looked over at Gemma. Her pale

appearance didn't strike him as hard as it would've struck other people because he was used to this look – along with the dark circles around her eyes and her chaffed lips. Leandra had the same look.

"I'm looking for something to cook for dinner."

"And Gianna approved this?" Gemma asked.

"Approved?" He smirked. *Approved. That's funny.*

"She doesn't allow me to cook a thing," Gemma told him. "She doesn't even like it when I heat up soup in the microwave." Gemma coughed.

"Have you eaten?"

"Not since lunch. I was just about to warm up some soup since Gianna ain't down here yet to stop me."

"Well, now *I'm* down here to stop you. Have a seat, Gemma. I got it."

"You really don't have to, Ramsey. I know you're doing the whole win-the-little-sister-over-to-impress-the-big-sister-thing, but it's really not necessary."

"I know, especially since big sister is already impressed by me."

Gemma smiled. "Why do you think that?"

"I don't think it. I know it. Now, you have a seat, little lady, and let me prepare some soup for you."

"Okay."

Ramsey walked over to the pantry and removed a can of soup. Looking at the label, he asked her, "Is clam chowder okay?"

"Yes. That's fine."

He poured it into a bowl and put it in the microwave. After three minutes on high, he stirred it, then put it on the table in front of her. "Don't burn yourself."

"Thank you, Ramsey."

"You're welcome."

He returned to the refrigerator and stood there, trying to piece together a meal in his head. He didn't do this – coordinate meals. Carson cooked his meals. He never had to give much thought to things like this before.

"Um, may I make a suggestion?" Gemma asked.

He looked back at her with the refrigerator door still open. "What's that?"

"If you can't cook, which I highly suspect that you can't, why don't you just run down the street to get something?"

"Because I'm afraid your sister won't let me back in."

Gemma giggled. "She's mad at you, huh?"

"Something like that."

"I told you she'd freak out if she woke up to find you in her bedroom."

"Yeah. You did warn me."

"But, no worries. You can run out and pick up some food. I'll let you back in."

"And what if you're asleep?"

"Oh. Right."

"Well, in that case, order a pizza."

"Good thinking, Gemma. Tell me what kind your sister likes."

"She likes meat. Pepperoni, sausage,

bacon..."

"Gotcha." He pulled out his phone and called the nearest pizza restaurant, confirming delivery in twenty-five minutes.

"Gemma, I told you I would heat up your soup," Gianna said sternly as soon as she walked into the kitchen.

"Ramsey heated it up for me."

Gianna glared at Ramsey, then quickly looked away.

"Hmm...I'm picking up some tension here," Gemma said.

"I'm not trying to cause any tension," Ramsey said. "Just trying to help." He pulled out a chair, sat across from Gemma but kept his eyes on Gianna. She was filling a cup with ice and water. Her hair was pinned up like it usually is when she had to work. She had on jeans and had changed out of a blouse into a gray T-shirt, nothing fancy but still it shaped her body well. She kept her back to him while she drank water. He took it as her ignoring him. She wanted to ignore him? Fine. He'd talk to Gemma. He looked across the table at her and asked, "What do you think about a having a full-time nurse, Gemma?"

Gianna frowned, turned around to look at him but didn't say a word.

"I told you, last night, I couldn't afford that," Gemma replied.

"And we don't need your help, Ramsey," Gianna said.

"That's exactly what someone who needs help, but is in denial would say," he said, looking at her. Returning his attention to Gemma, he asked, "Gemma, what if money was no object? Don't you think a home nurse would greatly help you and Gianna? It would free up Gianna so she doesn't have to worry so much while she's at work. I mean, use today for an example. She didn't work at all because she had to take you to the hospital. If you had a nurse, Gianna could've been working."

Gianna's temples pulsated. Jaw hardened. "Don't talk about me like I'm not standing here."

He narrowed his eyes at her. "Then I advise you get in on this discussion and act like you *are* standing there."

"It *would* help us, Gianna," Gemma said. "I told Ramsey we had looked into it, and—"

"And she said you couldn't afford it," Ramsey finished saying. "Sorry for interrupting, Gem."

Gem? He was on a nickname basis with her sister now?

"That's okay," Gemma told him.

"We *can't* afford it, and that's really none of your concern, Ramsey," Gianna said, then took a sip of water.

Ramsey smiled. None of his concern...he'd be the judge of that.

When the doorbell rang, he got up and said, "That's probably the pizza."

"You ordered a pizza?" Gianna asked, her forehead gradually creasing.

"Yep," Ramsey said. "It was Gemma's idea."

Gianna glared at her smiling sister, watching

as Gemma blew her a kiss. She caught the air kiss and pitched it back at her.

As the doorbell sounded again, Ramsey headed there. Gianna brushed past him while saying, "You don't know if it's the delivery guy so move out the way."

He laughed. "Slow down, sweetness."

"No. This is *my* house. I'll get the door in my own house."

"Are you expecting company?"

"No."

"Then, it's probably the pizza."

"You don't know that." Gianna snatched the door open to see the pizza delivery guy standing there with one box.

Ramsey's grin widened. He took his wallet from the back pocket of his slacks, then handed the driver a twenty dollar bill. "Keep the change, man."

"Thanks," the delivery man said. "You all have a good evening."

"You do the same," Ramsey told him while Gianna stomped back to the kitchen.

Moments later, he set the pizza on the table. "Where are your plates?"

Leaned against the counter, Gianna crossed her arms. "You don't know by now? I figured since you're trying to play man-of-the-house, you'd already know where everything was."

His eyes narrowed. "Are you always this grouchy when you wake up from a nap?"

Gemma snickered, then covered her mouth trying to disguise laughter.

"I'm not grouchy."

"She's really not," Gemma said, lying through her teeth. It took Gianna a minute to get her bearings after a nap more so than other people. "She's just not used to having a man in the house. Or in her life. Like, ever." Gemma laughed.

Searching the cabinets for plates, Ramsey chuckled. "Good one, Gemma," he said, then winked at her. "Aha...see I didn't need your help after all, sweetness. Found them."

"Stop calling me sweetness."

"Stop being sweet and I will," he said, placing three plates on the table.

"How can I be grouchy and sweet at the same time?"

"Why don't you tell me?"

Still leaning against the counter, Gianna rolled her eyes. Okay, so she was grouchy when she woke up from a nap. She wasn't one of those *Skip to My Lou* morning people. But she also wasn't accustomed to a man crowding her space and being all up in her way. She didn't care how fine he was. How kind he was. How charming, well-built, handsome and any other word you would think of to describe a man as fine as Ramsey St. Claire. She just wasn't in the mood for this, especially not after the day she had.

"Gemma, do you want to try a small slice?" Ramsey asked her.

"No. I better not. I'll end up with heartburn. Plus, the doctor said I should be eating healthy nutritious food and it ain't nothing healthy about all that grease and cheese."

"Right," Ramsey said. "Under normal circumstances, I wouldn't indulge either, but..." *Desperate times calls for desperate measures.* "Gianna, how many slices would you like?"

"I'll get it myself," she grumbled.

"No, please have a seat."

"Ramsey, I said I got it," Gianna reiterated.

"No, *I* got it. Have a seat. You've had a long day. Let me serve you. Please."

She sighed heavily but finally sat down as he had requested. She didn't want to, but she did. And she deserved to. She was tired. Exhausted. A full week of sleep wouldn't be enough rest to cure her tiredness from going nonstop, working hard for her sister – going to appointments and putting in time at the bakery. It wasn't for herself. It was all for Gemma. Now that she finally had a break – finally had someone to take some of the weight off of her shoulders – she didn't know what to do with herself. She was the one who was supposed to be preparing dinner right now, warming Gemma's soup, serving her a glass of cold water before preparing her own meal. Right now, she was just sitting at the table, doing nothing but staring at a brown pizza box. She wasn't accustomed to somebody else stepping in and taking over. Serving her.

When Ramsey set a plate in front of her, she blinked out of her thoughts and caught a whiff of his cologne. Why did he always smell so good? Did all men smell this good? Did—?

"You don't know?" Ramsey asked, looking at Gianna as he stood in front of the refrigerator with the door wide open. She was frowning, and he didn't know why his question warranted a frown.

Why is he looking at me? Is he talking to me? "Don't know what?" she asked.

"I asked you what you wanted to drink. Coke, Fruit Punch, tea...um, what else do you have in here?" he said, scanning the contents of the refrigerator.

"Coke is fine."

"Little ice or a lot of ice?" he asked.

I could get it myself for all this... Her jaw twitched.

"Sorry. I don't know you well enough to know how you like your drinks yet."

Yet? "Just make it the way you would prepare yours."

"Okay. One Coke with a *lot* of ice, coming right up."

Gianna shook her head. She glanced at Gemma, watching her smile.

"Isn't this nice of him to do this for you, Gianna," Gemma whispered. "Enjoy."

Enjoy? Yeah. Right. She didn't know how it felt to enjoy anything. Well, she used to enjoy baking and designing cupcakes until her passion for it turned into a chore. Until it became something she *had* to do to make ends meet and lately, ends hadn't been meeting at all. How could she be passionate about something when she had to worry about paying bills, or wonder when the repo man was going to show up to take her car? And there was no doubt about it – she didn't know when or where, but repo dude was going to show up. She hadn't paid a car note in three months.

"Here you are," he said, placing a glass on the table and sitting next to her. He looked at her, eyes following the curve of her jaw on down to her lips. "Is everything to your liking?"

She could see him staring at her via her peripherals. "Yes. It's fine. Thanks."

"You're welcome." Ramsey picked up a slice of pizza and nearly took half of it into his mouth. "Mmm...I haven't had pizza in a while."

"We *just* had Stromboli last night," Gianna said.

"Stromboli isn't pizza," he mumbled.

"It sure tasted like pizza."

He stopped chewing and looked over at her, just staring with a chunk of pizza stuffed in his jaw. Maybe she *was* cranky and grumpy when she woke up from naps. Okay, he'd have to get used to that since he was the complete opposite. *Nothing you can't handle, Ramsey. You've closed million-dollar deals. Putting up with a little attitude should be a breeze. Besides, she's not like this all the time.*

Turning his attention away from her, he resumed eating, then washed down the first slice of pizza with a gulp of Coke. "This is probably not the right time to bring this up, but I think it would be a good thing to hire a nurse for Gemma. That way, you can work without worries, knowing that Gemma will be well taken care of."

Gianna's insides churned with irritation. "What part of *we can't afford this* don't you understand?"

"What part of me telling you that you can *use* me however you like, don't you understand?"

Gemma's eyebrows went up as she looked up at her sister. Gianna hadn't touched her pizza. She was just sitting there, and Gemma could see how uncomfortable she was, and she knew why. Ramsey was staring at Gianna. Hard. They were already sitting close, but he was making it more uncomfortable with his direct, heated gaze that wouldn't let up.

Gianna pulled in a breath – one that she hoped would give her a speck of courage – and turned to look at him. Her eyes met his attentive, concerning ones briefly, before rolling down the bridge of his nose. To his mustache. His lips.

Lawd have mercy...

"Um..." she cleared her throat after looking away from him, staring down at her plate – at the untouched slice of pizza on her plate to be more specific. "I heard you when you said I could...could, um...*use* you, whatever that means, but—"

"I already hired a nurse, Gianna," Ramsey interrupted to say. "She wants to come by tomorrow after you get off work to meet Gemma."

Her breath hitched. "Wait...you got somebody coming to *my* house without discussing it with me, first?"

"That's what I'm doing now," he said, watching her brow raise. "I'm discussing it with you."

"But it's after the fact. You've already done it, now you want to discuss it? And let's not forget that I *did not* ask for your help."

"You didn't have to ask. I know you needed it, so I stepped in to assist."

"And what are you getting out of this, Ramsey?"

He looked at her. Smirked. "The nurse's name is Harriet. She'll be here tomorrow around seven-thirty."

"Sounds cool to me," Gemma said. "Think about how much this will free you up, Gianna."

Gianna felt her stomach churn. She was too queasy to snap the way she wanted to. So she said the first thing that popped into her head. "Get out, please."

"You want me to leave?" he asked.

"Yes. I want you to leave."

Gemma frowned. "Gianna, what are you—?"

"It's alright, Gemma," Ramsey told her. He took a napkin from the table and wiped his mouth before he stood up. "Enjoy the rest of your evening, ladies."

He continued on to his Range, sat there and wrapped his fingers around the steering wheel, squeezing. Gianna was proving to be stubborn – something he hadn't expected. Any other woman would be showering him with praise of thanks, but not Gianna Jacobsen. He couldn't say he was surprised. Gianna wasn't like other women, he knew, and thus, he had major ground to cover before Friday – before Felicity presented her with his proposal. Currently, he was off to a bad start.

* * *

"I THINK YOU were too hard on him, Gianna," Gemma said. "He's only trying to help us."

"Yeah, well, I didn't ask him for any help, did I?"

"You didn't, which should make his display of kindness even more meaningful. Out of the kindness of his heart, he's trying to help you—help us—and you're pushing him away like we don't need the help. Why are you being so stubborn, Gianna?"

"Because people don't just go around helping folk for free and out of the kindness of their hearts anymore."

"Yeah, they do."

"No, they don't, Gem. If somebody does something nice for you, especially unsolicited—supposedly out of the *kindness* of their heart—they want *something* in return and you can take that to the bank. That's how the cookie crumbles, lil' girl."

Lil' girl... Gemma shook her head.

"Besides, I've been taking care of you for my entire life, Gemma Marie Jacobsen, and I never had any help. Why do I need it now?"

"Gianna..." Gemma's eyes swam with tears. "I know it's been hard, okay. I know you don't want me to know how difficult it's been for you, but I *know* it's been hard." With her voice trembling to pieces, she continued, "You don't complain because you don't want me to know how bad things are and it's because of me. It's all my fault because of my diagnosis. I'm a burden to—"

"No you're not," Gianna interjected, trying to embrace her sister but Gemma nudged her away.

"I am. I *know* I am and I'm sorry for pu..." Gemma sobbed but got herself together enough to say, "I'm sorry for putting you through this. I truly am. I wish I could step in like Ramsey and help you out, but I can't." Her lips trembled. "I don't have the means to. I can't even stay awake for and extended period, so what am I supposed to do to help you? Huh?"

"I don't expect you to help me, Gemma."

"I know you don't. What I'm saying is, if I could, I would. Since I can't, why not let someone who has the heart and the means help you instead of being so hard on the man? He genuinely wants to help us. Let him." Gemma brushed tears away from her eyes. "I'm going to lay down now. Goodnight, Gianna."

"Wait," Gianna said before Gemma walked away. She embraced her sister, feeling her body tremble as she cried in her arms. "I love you, Gemma."

"I love you, too, Gianna."

"We'll be okay," she said. "Everything will be okay, sweet girl."

"Okay," Gemma said softly.

Chapter 4

WHAT A DAY...

Gianna returned home exhausted. Her neck was stiff. Her lower back aching. Her feet were crying, begging for mercy and overall, she just felt like a glob of tiredness. She was more tired than normal since she had the day off yesterday. Well, she still worked somewhat, having to take Gemma to the doctor and all, but she didn't have to be on her feet like she had to be at the bakery. And, the bakery had been a lot busier than normal – good for her empty wallet – bad for her poor feet. That's why, as soon as she arrived home, she prepared a pot of vegetable beef stew and placed it on the stove. While that cooked, she relaxed in a hot shower for ten minutes and afterward, massaged her feet before dressing in a pair of light gray cotton shorts with the matching tank top, then sliding her feet into a pair of fuzzy socks. She let her hair hang loose, massaged her scalp where the ponytail holder was and shook her hair free, releasing tension everywhere she could in her body.

Back downstairs, she checked the pot, stirring the boiling stew – the aroma of peas, onions, carrot, celery, corn, beef and broth filling the house. Now that she was situated and somewhat relaxed, she walked to Gemma's bedroom, opened the door and saw her lying there with her eyes opened. The lamp on her nightstand was turned on.

"Hey," Gemma said, rubbing her eyes.

"Hey, Gem."

Gemma yawned and stretched her arms up high. "When did you get in?"

"The usual time. I'm making a stew."

"I know. That glorious scent is what woke me up."

Gianna smiled. "Good. Come on to the kitchen. I'll give you some as soon as it gets done."

Gemma stretched again and stood up, following Gianna to the kitchen. "How was the bakery?" she asked, her question hidden in a yawn.

"Super busy." Gianna walked over to the pantry to grab a loaf of honey-wheat bread. "I was baking cupcakes left and right. It was definitely a profitable day."

"Cool. That's great. I wish..." Gemma's thoughts were interrupted by a long cough.

Gianna turned around to look at her, then came to her aid, pulling out a chair at the table for her to sit down and then quickly getting a glass of water. "Here. Drink," she said, holding the glass to her mouth.

Gemma took a sip, then cleared her throat.

"That cough seems to be getting worse since yesterday. I'm taking you back to the doctor tomorrow."

"No. I'm fine. Let me just sit here for a moment and sip on this water. My throat's kinda dry. That's all."

When the doorbell rang, Gianna frowned. She wasn't expecting anyone. She walked to the door and peered through the peephole. She saw a woman who looked middle-aged, a little on the thick side with curly black hair. She didn't recognize the lady. What was she doing? Selling something? Before she opened the door, Gianna asked, "Who is it?"

"It's Harriet. Are you Gianna?" the woman called out.

Harriet? The nurse Harriet? The woman Ramsey hired to watch after Gemma without her permission? Gianna opened the door to greet Harriet. "Hi. Yes, I'm Gianna. Come in."

When Harriet stepped inside, Gianna said, "Um...did Ramsey not call you to cancel this?"

"Cancel?" Harriet asked, a look of confusion touching her features. "No. I just got off the phone with him. He told me he was ten minutes away, and that was five minutes ago."

"Ten minutes away? From here?"

"Yes. He's meeting me since I don't know you. This *is* the right place, isn't it? Are you the woman with the sister named Gemma?"

"Yes but—"

The doorbell rang.

Gianna inhaled a breath and went back to the door again. When she opened it, Ramsey was standing there with a smile on his face. A twinkle in his eyes.

After she kicked him out yesterday, he could

still stand there and smile at her? And that cute dimple of his was on full display. His chocolate, late evening skin looked as delicious as a Godiva truffle. And he smelled so doggone good... *Ahhhh.* She licked her lips in appreciation.

"Hi, Gianna," he said.

"Hey, Ramsey. Um...listen...about yesterday—"

"Don't worry about yesterday. Yesterday's history."

"No, it's not. Well, it is but I..." Gianna stepped outside, pulling the door closed behind her to give them some privacy. "I need to say this. I'm sorry about what I said to you yesterday and how I was behaving. I was tired and upset. It's no excuse and I realize you were trying to help me and I was being rude to you. I don't want you to think that I'm ungrateful because I appreciate everything. I do. I just don't feel comfortable letting people help me with stuff and I don't like taking money from you."

"I didn't give you any money."

"No, but you leave me excessive tips whenever you're in the bakery, paid Gemma's copay for the doctor visit yesterday, you bought my groceries, you ordered dinner for me several times and now you're hiring this nurse. It's just like giving me money, isn't it?"

He smiled and took her hands into his, feeling the undercurrent of her nerves flow through her soft fingers.

Gianna was too nervous to look at him, so

she looked down, where their hands met.

"Gianna, just say thank you," he said wanting to stroke her hair and nudge her chin up so she would lock eyes with him. He fought the urge to.

"But—"

"Just say, thank you."

An endearing smile appeared on her face. "Thank you."

"You're welcome. Now, let's go inside so I can introduce you to Harriet." Ramsey reached for the door and pulled it open.

"Do you know her personally?"

"In a way. She's a friend of my mother's," he said, closing the door as they entered the house.

They continued on to the kitchen to see that Harriet was quick to start working. She was standing at the stove, stirring the stew.

"I didn't want it to get scorched," she said, glancing over to Gianna. "I hope you don't mind."

"No, not at all. Thank you."

"You're welcome, dear," Harriet said.

"So, Harriet, you've met Gemma," Ramsey said.

Harriet looked at Gemma. "Yes, I have. We're going to get along just fine."

"That's good to hear," Ramsey said, looking at Gianna. "As I was telling you, Gianna, Harriet is a friend of my mother's."

"Yes," Harriet said. "Me and Bernadette go way back. I used to be Ramsey's grandmother's caretaker until she passed away."

Ramsey nodded. "Harriet is a certified nurse aide. She knows CPR, the Heimlich maneuver...she can do it all. And she'll take Gemma back and forth to her appointments. Is that okay with you, Gemma?"

Gemma nodded. "Yep."

"And I'll cook, clean...I'm here to make both of your lives easier," Harriet said. "Ramsey has already given me an overview of what a typical day for you is like."

"A typical day for—for me?" Gianna asked, glancing at Ramsey.

He winked at her. Smiled.

"Yes, Gianna," Harriet replied. "I took the liberty of making a schedule." Harriet searched through her shoulder bag and pulled out a notebook, reading off plans for Gemma. She'd already written detailed, daily schedules that included a variety of activities so Gemma could get out during the day and not lie around sleeping for hours upon hours at a time. She needed this. To stay active in conjunction with healthy eating.

"This is...wow. This is just what Gemma needs, Harriet."

"Perfect," Harriet said. "When should I start?"

"Um...uh..."

"I'm available tomorrow if you would like me to start right away," Harriet said.

"That'll be fine with me," Gemma chimed in to say.

Gianna smiled nervously. "Okay, then I guess I'm fine with it."

"Good," Ramsey said bringing his hands to a clap. "Gianna, what time do you head to the bakery in the mornings? I told Harriet between seven and seven-thirty."

"Yeah. That's when I usually leave."

"Okay, so Harriet, to be on the safe side, can you be here at seven?" Ramsey asked.

"I sure can. Oh, and I'll take care of breakfast and everything. You don't have to worry about a thing, Gianna."

Ramsey looked at Gianna and saw the moment her chest rose and lowered slowly.

"It's okay, Gianna." Ramsey threw an arm around her, pulling her close to him.

"I know. I'm just a little nervous," she replied. "Thank you so much, Harriet."

"You're welcome."

"Can you stay for dinner?" Gianna asked.

"Oh, honey, I already cooked, but thanks for the offer." Harriet slid the folder back into her bag.

"I haven't eaten," Ramsey said with his arm still around Gianna. Then lowering his mouth to her ear, he whispered, "I don't hear you inviting me to dinner."

Gianna blushed and felt warm all over at his whisper. "Okay, Ramsey. Would you like to stick around for dinner?"

"I would love to, Cupcake."

Harriet smiled. She could see right away that Ramsey had a fondness for Gianna. "Well, I guess I'll be on my way."

"Thanks again for stopping by, Harriet," Gianna said.

"Yes. Thank you, Harriet," Gemma added.

"You're welcome," Harriet responded as Gianna opened the door for her, watching as she headed down the stairs and to her car. Gianna closed the door after Harriet drove off.

Back in the kitchen now, she watched as Ramsey stirred the stew. She smirked. "And just what do you think you're doing with your non-cooking self?"

He glanced back at her. "Just stirring. It's about all I can do when it comes to food."

"Somehow, I doubt that." Gianna looked at Gemma. She was quiet and her arms were crossed like she was cold. "Are you okay, Gem?"

"Yeah, but I think I'll take my soup to my room. Can you...can you fix me a bowl?"

"Sure, babycakes."

Gianna took a bowl from the cabinet and added a serving of stew to it. Then she walked to the table and helped Gemma up.

"Goodnight, Ramsey," Gemma said. "I'll probably pass out after I finish this soup."

Ramsey cracked a smile. "Goodnight, Gemma."

Once she was inside of her bedroom, Gemma said softly to Gianna, "Okay, I'm not all *that* tired...just wanted you two to have some time alone to talk."

"You sneaky, little rascal," Gianna said, amused.

"Now, go. Talk and keep that weird crap you do at bay."

Gianna shook her head as Gemma sat on the

bed. "You ought to be ashamed of yourself, Gemma."

"You ought to be thanking your lucky stars that this man has come into your life."

Gianna briefly reflected on that. Ramsey was a customer and now, he was a – a friend. "Enjoy your stew. If you need anything, just yell."

"I won't need anything," Gemma said smiling all sneaky. "Now get back out there, Stella, and try to get your groove back. Well, you can't get back what you never had, so just, um...just try to do something. Good grief." Gemma laughed.

Gianna smirked, shook her head and continued towards the door.

Ramsey's eyes locked on her as soon as she stepped into the kitchen. "Is she okay?"

"Yeah, she's fine." Gianna washed her hands, then started preparing grilled cheese sandwiches.

Leaning against the counter with his legs crossed at the ankles, he watched her work.

She glanced over at him. "So, you really don't know how to cook?"

"No. I have a live-in housekeeper, who's also my cook. And he runs errands for me. Schedules appointment. I guess maybe you can call him my personal assistant."

"And you have another assistant at work?"

"A secretary. Yes."

"Right," Gianna said, placing a skillet on the stove after which she added a spoonful of butter. She added two cheese sandwiches to the pan and let both sides of the bread cook until they were golden brown. Then after those two sandwiches were finished, she added two more, allowing them to brown to perfection before turning the stove off. She filled two bowls with stew and brought them over to the table.

Ramsey walked there and sat down.

"What would you like to drink, Ramsey?" He looked over at her as she stood near the refrigerator. Would he ever get tired of hearing her say his name?

"Ramsey?"

"Water will be fine."

She also got water for herself, then walked over to the table.

"Thank you," he said.

"You're welcome."

She tasted the stew, deciding to sprinkle in a little salt and pepper. Then she broke off a piece of the grilled cheese sandwich, dipped it into the bowl and took a bite.

"Ah, so that's how you do it. Okay." Ramsey copied her, taking his first bite of the only meal he'd ever eaten of hers. Well, he had her cupcakes before, but that wasn't a meal. Plus, as it turned out, most people who could bake cakes and pastries weren't necessarily good at cooking *real* food. Gianna proved to be one of those people who could do both. "This is outstanding."

She grinned. "It's not all that."

"It is. Who taught you how to cook?"

"I taught myself. I learned how to bake from the bakery I worked at prior to opening my own bakery." Gianna watched him chew, enraptured by the movement of his mouth – his lips – but when he glanced up at her, she looked away, stirred her soup and began eating again.

"Speaking of the bakery, how was work today?" he inquired.

"It was busy. I was baking nonstop."

"Oh yeah?"

"Yep."

"What was the cupcake of the day?"

"Strawberry shortcake. I sold thirty-six in one hour. That's like a new record for me. I don't think I've ever been so busy."

He took a sip of water. "That's good though, right?"

"Wait...what did you do, Ramsey?"

He laughed. "What do you mean?"

"Your dimple is showing and you look like you've been up to something."

"Is that right?" he asked. "You know me well enough to know when I'm up to something?"

Playfully narrowing her eyes, she asked, "What did you do?"

He took another sip of water. "I may have taken out a few ads for the bakery in *Charlotte Magazine* and *The Observer*."

Her eyes brightened. "You *may* have?"

"Okay. I did."

"Why?" she asked excitedly, but thoroughly confused. Felicity was the only person who helped her out with bakery-related work. No one else. For him to step in and do these things for her – to help her mop floors, sweep and now take out ads – was blowing her mind.

He shrugged and ate the last of his grilled cheese. "Do you mind if I get another?"

"I'll get it for you," Gianna said, standing.

"No. Sit down. Eat. I'll get it...may as well get some more stew while I'm up." He walked over to the stove where she'd left the sandwiches and asked, "Would you like another?"

"No, thanks. I can usually get through one bowl with one grilled cheese."

When he sat down again, she looked at him and asked, "I'm not letting you off the hook. Why are you doing all of this, Ramsey? One thing I *did* learn from my mother was, ain't nothing free in this world. So, tell me...what do you want?" She sipped water while waiting for his answer.

And she waited. And waited...

"Well?" she asked.

He hesitated – not for himself but for her – because he knew she wouldn't expect the answer he was going to give. But her inquisitive brown eyes wanted an answer, so he was going to give it to her. "You," he finally said.

"Huh?" she asked, before taking the last spoonful of soup.

"I said, I want you."

Gianna choked, leaned forward with her left hand on her chest and the right covering her mouth.

"Are you okay?" Ramsey asked, standing.

Gianna was steadily coughing, heaving.

"Gianna?"

She held up a finger while still coughing a

little. When she was able to clear her passageway again, she said roughly, "I'm fine." She wiped her mouth with a napkin.

"Are you sure?"

"Yes. I'm sure. Your answer just took me off guard."

He sat down again but didn't touch his food. He just looked at her. "Since you're fine, let's talk about it. What if what I wanted was you, Gianna?" he asked with arrogance in his eyes.

"Stop playing games with me. You already made me choke once."

"Why won't you answer the question?"

"Because it's absurd."

"It's not absurd. Your friend Felicity has turned this very idea into a business and sold it to prospective clients. It can't be all that bizarre, now can it?"

"Either way it goes, I don't know you like that, and you don't know me well enough to know if you *want* me...whatever that means. And Felicity's business is Felicity's business. It has nothing to do with me."

"I see." His eyebrows raised briefly before he started eating again, taking spoon after spoon to his mouth. She would find out soon enough that her friend's business *did* have something to do with her, especially after Felicity met with her on Friday.

Deciding to test the limits of his persuasion, he said, "A moment ago, I told you I wanted you. Are you telling me I can't have you?"

Her palm was so sweaty, the spoon slid right out of her grasp. "Describe your definition of want?"

He stared at her lips when he responded, "You know. Want."

"As in?" she probed further.

As in I want you and all the peculiar ways that come along with the package. I want to stare at your face until you dissolve into my mind. I want to smell you. Bathe in the aroma of your sweetness. To kiss those sweet lips. To hold you close to me like I did last night, but I don't want to hold you for only one night. I want you forever. I want to laugh with you. Cry with you. I want to be the man you run to. I want to be your rock. Your protector. Your provider. I want whatever your heart desires.

"Okay. I'll be more specific," Ramsey said. "I want you for companionship."

"That encompasses a lot, don't you think?"

You have no idea. "Yes, it does."

Gianna glanced at him and looked away. For some reason, she was seeing in his eyes things he wouldn't say. She could tell, right away, that he was holding back. "Well, I couldn't do something like that."

"We're doing it right now. Sharing a meal together. Companionship. We shared a meal last night. Companionship. You fell asleep in my arms." *And that was the best feeling in the world.*

"You're right. I did, but I don't have time for companionship or dating, or anything related to the two."

"Because you never make time for yourself." He wiped his mouth after finishing up the second bowl of stew.

"You're right. I'll acknowledge that. I don't make time for myself."

"Do you think that's fair?"

"Fair?" she asked, meeting his direct gaze. Breaking away from it, she stood up to collect their bowls. While taking them to the sink, she asked, "When has anything in life ever been fair? Besides, I don't have time to think about myself when my sister is—" She stopped short of saying *dying*, but somehow she felt Ramsey knew where she was going. Changing the subject, she turned around and asked, "Didn't you say you lived in Lake Norman?"

"Yes, but not *in* the actual lake. The city."

"I know that, silly." A smile grew on her face.

He liked that. That's what he was aiming for. A smile.

"You drove all the way here from Lake Norman, just to introduce me and Gem to Harriet?"

"Yes. I make the drive all the time since my business is here."

"I know, but I'm talking about today. You're off work, so you really didn't have to drive here just to introduce us."

"I know. I did it because I wanted to. Because I like you, and I got dinner out of the deal, so I see it as a win-win."

Gianna smiled. "Well, I hate to put you out, but I have to get up early tomorrow for work."

Ramsey rolled his arm to glance at his watch. "It's only a few minutes after nine."

"Yeah, and I still need to shower and get to

bed. I'm sure I'll have a busy day tomorrow thanks to you."

"I'm sure you will," Ramsey said standing. He walked over to where she'd been standing – by the sink. He didn't sneak up on her this time. In fact, she was watching him, scrutinizing him as he approached as if readying herself for whatever it was she anticipated he'd do. "May I hug you?"

Her face flushed. "Umm...let me think about it."

"You don't have time to think. You're kicking me out, remember? Now, can I get my hug, please?" he asked, taking another step forward.

"You may," she answered. If she could handle being in his arms last night, couldn't she tolerate a brief hug? Then again, she was asleep last night. Right now, she was wide awake, fully aware of what was about to happen.

Help me, Jesus.

When his thick, muscly arms closed around her, her senses fully awakened at the feel of his strength capturing her. At his body reeling her in. He squeezed her firmly to his chest. Her body shook, but not enough to where she would be embarrassed. And it wasn't her fault he was so freakin' handsome. That he was a tower of muscles. That his pheromones rendered her weak-kneed.

"Have a good night's rest, sweetness."

"I'll try," she said as he released her. "You have a good night, too, driving back in the lake—I mean to the lake. To Lake Norman."

"I will." *And I'll be thinking about you all the way home.*

Chapter 5

THE RAIN WASN'T slacking up which meant Gianna would have to make a run for the rear entrance of the bakery. She'd forgotten to bring an umbrella today. She was distracted, well more like excited that Harriet was at the house this morning, eager to take care of Gemma. And she'd been so busy telling Harriet where everything was, giving her reminders about Gemma's medication, that it slipped her mind to grab the umbrella from the coat closet. It wasn't raining when she left the house. The sky was actually misleading – partly sunny like there could be a slight chance of rain. The kind of weather where meteorologists claim there's a ten percent chance of rain just to cover their behinds but nothing usually happens.

Today, something happened. It was pouring buckets – raining so hard the drops pummeled the roof of her car like they were seeking entry. The ominous sky was varying colors of gray and thunder rumbled and clapped while lightning sliced through the darkness. It was morning time, almost eight o'clock, but it looked more like night.

Gianna sighed, searching her car for something she could use to cover her head.

This was one of those days that, as an adult, you should have the right to stay in bed if you wanted to like it was a Federal holiday. God knows she could've used the sleep. Now, she was about to get drenched trying to get inside the building. How was she going to work in soaked clothes?

"Okay, Gianna...you just have to make a run for it," she said, talking to herself – more like talking herself into doing it. She had a lot of work to do today, and she definitely couldn't get any of it done by sitting in the car. But she didn't want to get soaked on the way to the door. *Ugh.* She cringed at how uncomfortable it would be, but she had to do what had to be done. She didn't have much choice in the matter.

"Alright, Gianna...just make a run for it." She reached for the door handle and when she was just about to open the door, she saw a white SUV pull up next to her. Peering through the water-spotted window, she recognized the SUV as Ramsey's Range Rover. She saw the headlights go off so he must've turned off the engine but she couldn't tell. The rain was hissing too loud, thunder clapping angrily.

Still looking at the SUV, she watched him walk around it and towards her with a large umbrella – like one of those top-grade, heavy duty, Weather Channel umbrellas that meteorologists use when they're on storm chasing assignments. He pulled the door handle, opening her door.

"You look like you need to be rescued," he

said, holding the umbrella with his left hand and extending his right hand to help her out of the vehicle.

She could only smile. He *was* like a real-life guardian angel. He knew what she needed without her having to ask and somehow always managed to pop up at the right time.

Taking his hand, she said, "Yes, I do need to be rescued from this rain, but what are you doing here, Ramsey?"

"Rescuing you," he said, holding her hand securely in his. When she was standing next to him, he pushed the door closed behind her, and he continued holding her hand until they were at the back entrance of the bakery.

Gianna unlocked the door while Ramsey shielded her from the rain with his massive umbrella. Then she stepped inside. He stepped partially inside, lowered the umbrella, leaving it dripping by the back door. Then he walked further inside, into Gianna's office where she had placed her purse in a desk drawer, locked it and sat down, looking at her computer.

Ramsey leaned against the door frame, nearly filling the height of it. For a moment, he just watched her. Admired her in her element. Behind her desk, preparing to get to work.

Gianna could feel him staring, and something told her not to look up at him but she did so anyway, watching his slender lips curve to an out-of-this-world smile. She looked away, positioning her right hand on the computer mouse to open a new window – one in which she could check the cupcake of the day rotation. Still, she could feel the warm beams of his eyes on her.

"How did everything go with Harriet this morning?"

"Fine." Gianna checked the calendar. Cookies and cream cupcakes were in line to be the special for the day.

"Fine, and that's it?" he asked.

His question shifted her thoughts from cookies and cream to chocolate. To him. "Yes. Harriet was eager to start and Gemma is happy that Harriet's there to take some of the pressure off of me."

"That's good, right?" he asked, grimacing just barely as he tried to read her, hoping he'd pleased her with hiring Harriet. He couldn't quite determine if he had just yet.

"Right." Gianna looked away from her computer screen to glance up at him. Jeez. He looked *extra* good this morning for some reason. Maybe it was the way the black Polo seemed to amplify his muscles, firm pectorals and overall athletic form. Or it could've been those faded gray jeans he wore with quilted paneling on the knees and gold zippers lining the pockets. Then again, it might've been the fact that he smelled so good and fresh and was wearing some cologne that had hypnotic power. Who was she kidding? It was a combination of all of those things. He just had it like that, whatever *it* was. Swagger. That's what it was.

She watched his lips form into a killer-sexy smile, then remembered she'd been staring at him – probably the reason he was smiling. "Ramsey, what are you doing here?"

"I thought I'd come by and help you out today."

"Help me do what?"

"Work."

She shook her head. Cracked a smile. "You don't have to help me work. You said you took time off of *your* job. I know you didn't do that because of me. You did it because you needed a break. Am I right?"

"Yes. You're right."

"Okay, so go take you break. Relax. Go on a Caribbean cruise or something."

"I'll go if you come with me."

Gianna blushed, then shook her head. "Okay...let me try this another way. Rainy days are generally slow for the cupcake business and I only have two catering orders today."

"Then, I'll help you out with that, and do some other things around here that I think could use some improvement."

"She lifted a brow. Excuse me?"

"No offense, sweetness, but there are some changes that need to be made."

"I like my shop just the way it is, thank you very much. How would you like for me to roll up to St. Claire Architects and tell you everything I don't like? Or better yet, how about I drop in on one of your construction projects and tell the workers to follow my orders instead of yours?"

"They wouldn't listen to you."

"Thanks for saying that 'cause *I'm* not

listening to *you*. I like my bakery." She looked at her computer screen again.

Ramsey raised his brows, then left her office. He walked into the kitchen area of the bakery, looking around as if he was inspecting the place. Then he walked out to the front counter where the cash register sat and the display case. Again, he looked around, taking mental notes of everything he thought this place was missing. Maybe Gianna was too busy to actually consider those things. Or she was probably too close to the bakery to know what sort of things she was missing. But being that this wasn't his element, he could think outside of the box and while he didn't know how to make cupcakes, he did know how to run a business. And he felt that it was his duty to bring certain things to her attention.

When he heard her moving around in the kitchen, he went there watching her set a large silver bowl on the counter. "What's on tap for today?"

Wearing her black apron and hair net, she said, "I have to get started on the regular cupcakes first."

"Regular...which ones are those?"

She took another large bowl from the bottom rack of a metal shelf. "Chocolate and vanilla."

"Do you mind if I watch?"

"Do I have a choice?" Gianna asked.

"You do if my watching would make you nervous..."

"Everything about you makes me nervous."

"Why?"

"Hunh?" she asked, looking at him.

"You said everything about me makes you nervous," Ramsey told her.

"O-M-G...I thought I said that in my head. I didn't know I said it out loud. Jeez."

"It's no problem. I can do something else, if—"

"No, don't worry about it," Gianna said. "Have you ever cooked anything in your life?"

"Yes. I cooked Ramen noodles way back in college."

Gianna laughed. "Microwaved Ramen noodles doesn't qualify as cooking."

"I had to stir it, too. Does that count for something?" He offered a short laugh.

"In other words, I got my hands full with you."

"Yes, and I'm all yours. Teach me, baby."

Baby? When did she become his baby? She pulled in a breath and said, "Okay so to make vanilla cupcakes, I need to mix flour, baking powder and kosher salt together first. Why don't you get my other apron so you don't get your clothes dirty?"

"It's cool. I don't mind getting dirty. What do you want me to do? Stir this?"

"Yes, and I'll start on the next mixture— unsalted butter, granulated sugar, eggs and vanilla extract." Gianna used the mixer to blend the ingredients then said, "Okay, in a moment, I'll need you to add half of the flour mixture. Okay?"

"Yep. Got it."

She allowed the mixture to blend for another thirty seconds or so then said, "Okay. Pour half of the flour mix in here."

"Alright. Easy enough." Ramsey tilted the bowl, pouring the mixture in, looking at her the entire time he was doing so, enjoying the feeling of being this close to her. Of her sharing her work with him.

"Okay. That's good," she said, her eyes landing on his lips. "Next, I'll add a...a little whole milk—" She poured in the milk. "And now, you can pour the rest of the flour mix in."

After doing so, he said, "That wasn't all that difficult."

"No, it's not. It's just a certain order I like to follow when making cupcakes."

"I see."

"Since I showed you how to do this, does that mean I get a private lesson on architecture?"

"If you would like. You can get anything you want from me, Gianna." And he meant it. She could get anything, have anything, take anything and do anything as long as she knew she was his. Unfortunately, she didn't know that yet.

"Ramsey, can you grab two of the cupcake pans and those paper liners?" she asked, pointing to where the materials were.

"Sure." He set the pans on the counter close to the cupcake batter. "Should I go ahead and line them?"

"Look at you knowing what to do in advance," she said. "Yes, you can line them.

That will help me out greatly."

He proceeded with filling each twelve-tray cupcake pan with liners.

Gianna went to find a couple of ice cream scoops since it was the easiest tool for her to fill the cupcake liners with batter. As he finished lining the pans, she handed him an ice cream scoop and said, "You do that pan. I'll do this one, and this part is very important. Only fill each liner three-fourths of the way and make sure to put the same amount of batter in each liner so they all cook evenly Got it?"

"Yes, ma'am."

"Sorry. Do I sound bossy?"

"You do, and I like it. I'm quickly learning that there are so many different sides to you, Ms. Jacobsen."

"Not really."

"Yes. Really. I can see them."

"If you say so, Ramsey."

Once they both completed the pans, Gianna slid them into the heated oven. "What time is it?" she asked him.

"It's 8:45 a.m."

"Okay. I need to work on the cupcake of the day."

"Which is?"

"Cookies and cream."

"Ooh. I haven't tried one of those yet."

"Then you'll get to try one today."

"I can't wait," he said, looking towards the front of the restaurant again. "Gianna, do you have one of those neon, electric 'Open' signs?"

"No."

"Why not?"

She lifted a shoulder. "I don't think I need one."

"Well, I think you do. In fact, I *know* you do."

"How do you figure that?"

"When people are walking pass you bakery, they need some visual indication that you're open without relying on the small-printed *hours of operation* on your door. So you whip up those cupcakes. I'll be back."

"Where are you going?" she felt inclined to ask. His presence electrified her in every way, but it felt nice to have someone there with her in the morning, helping her prep for the day. By the way he looked at her, she could tell he was surprised she'd asked. Had he heard the desperation in her voice?

"I'm going to grab some things you need."

"I don't need anything, Ramsey."

With a sparkle in his eyes, he replied, "I'll be right back, sweetness."

"Okay."

* * *

WHILE RAMSEY WAS away, Gianna unlocked the door since she opened for business at nine. She went back to the kitchen to put two dozen chocolate cupcakes in the oven – the chocolate ones for the cookies and cream frosting then focused on her catering orders – four-dozen red velvet cupcakes for one order and two-dozen, vanilla with buttercream frosting topped with sprinkles for the other. She even whipped up the frostings she would need – crushed Oreos with cream cheese, chocolate buttercream, plain cream cheese and regular white frosting.

The red velvet and plain vanilla cupcakes were in the oven now and while she waited for them to bake, she began frosting the two dozen that Ramsey had helped her prepare earlier. She put them in the display case and then, walking over to the coffee station, she brewed a canister of decaf and regular.

When her phone rang, she jumped. Ramsey had unnerved her but he wasn't even there. What did she have to be so jumpy about?

She rushed to her office to get the cordless, thinking that it could've been Harriet. Was something wrong with Gemma?

She snatched the phone from the base to see that the caller was Felicity.

"Hey," she answered breathily.

"Um...Gianna?"

"Yeah. It's me."

"Why do you sound like you're out of breath?"

"Because I am. I thought you were...were Harriet," she said huffing for air.

"Who's Harriet?"

"Gemma's new nurse."

"Gemma has a nurse?"

"Yes. Today's her first day and I'm a little nervous about it."

"Well, I think that's great," Felicity said. She somehow knew Ramsey had something to do with Gemma having a nurse. It still baffled her that he was the man Gianna had gone out with. They were complete and total opposites. She couldn't fathom Gianna having to deal with a man like him – a man with all the confidence and intelligence in the world. Arrogance on fleek. "How is Gemma by the way?" Felicity asked.

"She's...um...I took her to the doctor on Monday. She's on a new medication now since the chemo didn't work."

"The chemo *isn't* working?"

"No," Gianna said. "And her hair is shedding so bad. I don't think she's going to make it much longer, Felicity."

"Don't say that, Gianna. You have to think positive. Even when you're in a bad situation that you can't see your way out of—you still have to think positive."

"I know. I'm trying. Anyway, I don't want to be up in here crying, so what about you? How are you doing? It feels like it's been ages since we've seen each other."

Felicity chuckled. "Yeah, and it's only been a week."

"That's all?"

"Yes, girl, but I'm doing okay. I do have a dilemma on my hands though."

"What's wrong?"

"I'll tell you more about it on Friday. Let's make a cupcake breakfast date. I'll be there say around nine-ish. Will that work?"

"Yeah. That'll be cool."

"Perfect. I'll see you on Friday, then."

"Okay. Hey, I gotta go. I hear the doorbell."

"Later, girlfriend."

"Later." Gianna placed her phone on the desk and walked to the front. Her mouth dropped open in disbelief.

"Like it?" Ramsey asked, holding a huge, neon-orange 'Open' sign. "I think it should hang facing the sidewalk. What do you think?"

"Ramsey, you shouldn't have."

"I hired a couple of guys to install it today. I think I can handle the other stuff myself."

"What other—?"

And he was out the door...

When he came back inside, he had a black chalkboard in his hand and a box of chalk in the other. He placed the items on the counter, went back outside and returned with a full crate of two percent milk in small cartons and a large mason jar that was about the size of a gallon milk jug.

"Ramsey, what is all this?"

"Things I think your bakery needs. I have a chalkboard so you can easily write the cupcake of the day special from day to day. I brought some milk because a lot of people don't like coffee and may want something besides water with their cupcakes—especially the kids. And the mason jar is for tips. Since you refuse to get one, I took the liberty of buying one myself."

"But—"

"You work hard, Gianna. You deserve to be tipped. You deserve a whole lot more but we'll stick to the tips for now."

And she thought her mind was blown

before...

Gianna swallowed deeply. "Uh...thank you."

"You're welcome," he said removing a pink, polka dot tag from his pocket that read *tips*. "Do you have any tape around here?"

"All I have is duct tape."

"That should work."

She was still standing there and hadn't moved an inch when he said, "Where is it?"

"Oh! I'll get it."

"Just tell me where it is and I'll go get it."

"Be right back," Gianna said, taking off. She walked to her office, found the tape in her desk drawer – not sure why it was there, but whatever – then returned to the front. She noticed Ramsey had already hung up the beautiful chalk display board and had written the word *welcome* at the very top of it. And he actually drew a picture of a cupcake that brought a smile to her face. Who would've ever thought the millionaire architect would know how to draw a cupcake? Well, he did design buildings for a living. Drawing was right up his alley, or was everything computerized nowadays?

"How does it look?" he asked.

Gianna came out of her thoughts and blinked back to reality. "It looks good. I like that little cupcake you drew on there."

He smiled, pleased with the glow of happiness on her face. "Do you?"

"Yes. You can actually draw."

He looked at the chalkboard. "Well, more like sketch. Every building I design, I sketch by hand first to give the client a visual of what they've expressed to me that they wanted."

"Neat," she said, still looking at the chalkboard. "I have to admit, this is a good idea, Ramsey. My head is always in a cloud of flour. I don't have the time to think about things like this."

"Well, that's why I'm here."

She looked at him, held his gaze and tried to fight the smile that fought to force its way to her face. She lost that battle and was even blushing now.

Ramsey saw the moment her face flushed and instead of staring any longer, he took a pink chalk and wrote: *Cupcake of the Day*. Beneath it, he wrote: *Cookies & Cream $3.99/each*.

"Wait...my cupcakes are $2.95."

"And in my opinion, underpriced. If you want to keep the regular cupcakes priced at $2.95, fine. But the cupcake of the day is a specialty cupcake that should be priced accordingly."

Crap. All of his suggestions made sense.

"You don't have to agree with me, Gianna. This is your bakery. I'm just giving you an outside perspective."

"You're right. I don't know why I didn't think of that." She walked behind the counter while he stayed put near the chalkboard. "Now, the milk, on the other hand, might be a problem."

"How so?"

"I don't have room in my fridge to store

milk."

"I presumed you wouldn't, so I bought a drink display case. It can go right there beside the coffee bar."

"And who's going to monitor this milk for expiration dates? I certainly don't have time for it."

"They all expire on the same date," he said. "And, you can add it to your inventory and issue a flag or some other kind of warning that the expiration date is approaching. You do have an inventory system, don't you?"

"Yes, but—"

The bell tinkled. They both glanced at the door, watching as a delivery man brought in a mini display refrigerator.

"You're right on time, my man," Ramsey said.

"Where do you want it to go?"

Ramsey instructed the man where to put it – beside the coffee station. Then he slid him a twenty-dollar tip.

About fifteen minutes after the delivery guy left, workers came to install the 'Open' display sign. Ramsey talked to them for a few minutes, then he went to the newly delivered refrigerator and filled it with the small milk cartons.

Gianna was busy frosting the first batch of cookies and cream cupcakes as well as filling the display case with them, along with the vanilla cupcakes – a dozen with white icing, half with sprinkles and another dozen with chocolate icing, half of those with sprinkles as well. Then she baked two dozen more vanillas, after which she began preparing lemon frosting.

The rain picked up again. Thunder rumbled. The lights flickered several times, but the bakery never lost power. It was almost ten o'clock when the first customers walked through the door – a woman and a little girl who looked to be three, maybe four years old. Her bright eyes were glued to the display case, especially to the vanilla sprinkles.

"Good morning," Gianna greeted them. "What can I get for you?"

The woman looked at the display case, then glanced at the chalkboard and said, "Let me get one of your cookies and cream cupcakes and one vanilla with sprinkles."

"For the vanilla, do you want the one with the white frosting or chocolate?"

"Chocolate!" the little girl said, jumping up and down.

"Okay. Chocolate it is," her mother said with a giggle. "Oh, also, I'll take a small coffee and one milk."

"Alright," Gianna said, not knowing what price she should charge for the milk. Off the top of her head, she decided to charge $1.29. She'd consult with Ramsey on the price later. Speaking of Ramsey, where'd he run off to?

After the woman paid for her order, Gianna placed a coffee cup on the counter, instructed the woman where the coffee, cream and sugar was and told her she could take a carton of milk from the display refrigerator. Then she walked to the back to find out what Ramsey was doing. She found him in the kitchen filling two cupcake pans, all pre-lined, with the red velvet batter. She withheld a smile.

"Hey," she said.

He looked up with the ice cream scoop in his hand. "Hey."

"I just had a customer buy milk. I didn't know what to charge for it."

"I would say about $1.39, maybe," he said, then resumed filling the pan, paying careful, meticulous attention to what he was doing.

"I charged $1.29."

"Close enough." He pulled the oven door open and placed the pans inside.

"So should I charge $1.29 or $1.39?" she asked.

Ramsey closed the oven door then walked over to her in a sexy stride that made her pupils dilate. She took a step backward when he stopped immediately in front of her. "Which do you think is the better price point?"

She glanced up at him, staring at his lips, then looking away, feeling embarrassed for always staring at the man's lips, but they looked so yummy, she couldn't much help it. No woman probably couldn't resist the urge to glance at them, or *him* for that matter. "Um, I...I guess $1.29."

"Okay, $1.29 it is, then." He pressed his lips together and somehow, there was still a smirk on his face.

"And I was thinking that the display fridge should probably go...um...behind the counter."

"Why?"

"Because with it out there by the coffee, people could just go grab a milk and drink it. At least if it was behind the counter, they'd have to pay for it first."

"You got a point. I'll move it."

"Just like that?" she asked, gazing into his eyes with her sparkling ones. "No back and forth debate with me?"

"No debate," he said, knowing he should probably step away from her now and let her focus on work. Instead, he was focusing on her mouth. He wanted it...wanted to kiss those lips, but would she want it? Would she panic and flip out? Probably so. Still, that didn't stop him from lowering his head to hers, caught up in the splendor of her beautiful eyes. And those alluring lips of hers...they had a magnetic pull on his like she was winning a game of tug of war. More like tug of lips.

The bakery's phone rang before their lips could touch. Without saying a word, she rushed to get away from him. She escaped to her office to get the phone, closing the door behind her in hopes that the alone time would give her a chance to regain her composure. When the phone rang again, she picked up the cordless receiver and said, "The Boardwalk Bakery. How can I help you?"

"Hi. I need to place an order."

"Okay. Will you be picking it up today?"

"Yes," the woman said. "What time do you close?"

Gianna glanced up when she heard the

sound of the doorknob turning. Ramsey pushed the door open, stepped inside of her office and closed the door behind him. Suddenly her already small office felt tiny, especially with her undeniable attraction to him and his insistence on her *using* him any way she liked – not to mention they'd almost kissed just a minute ago.

"Hello?" the woman said.

"Oh, sorry," Gianna said coming out of her trance with Ramsey to focus on the phone call. "We close at seven."

Ramsey moved a folder on her desk so he could sit on the edge of it.

Gianna swallowed hard. He could've just sat in the chair next to her desk, but no. He just had to sit his firm, muscular backside *on* her desk. Any closer and he'd sidle right onto her lap.

"You close at seven?" the woman asked.

"Ye-yes. Seven o'clock."

"Perfect. I need to order four dozen carrot cupcakes. I can pick them up around five-ish."

"Okay," Gianna said scribbling a note to which she could see Ramsey reading as she wrote it. "I can have them ready by then. And your name?"

"Colette Wright."

"Okay. Thank you for your order, Colette. It will be ready for pick up at five."

"Perfect. See you then."

When Gianna hung up, Ramsey said, "Four dozen carrot cupcakes, huh?"

"Yes. Four dozen carrot cupcakes."

"Alright." He stood up, rubbing his hands together. "We can handle it."

"We?" She smiled, standing up.

"Yes. You and me, baby."

Baby...

She was his *baby* again?

"I can handle the register and you can stay back in the kitchen and work if that's okay."

"Are you sure, Ramsey? Working the register isn't as easy as it sounds."

"I got it. There's nothing I can't or won't handle for you."

She nibbled on her lip. *Gosh, I wish he would stop talking that way.* Stepping around him, she reached for the doorknob when she felt the warmth of his body shield her like a blanket from behind. His torso was pressed right up against her back, and then his hand covered hers, moving it away from the doorknob.

"Is there anything else you need me to do, Gianna?"

She thought she would die right then and there of a claustrophobic, body-quivering nervous system malfunction. Ramsey had her boxed in, his body folding to the slight bend of hers. And he was inhaling long breaths. She heard him do this several times. Was he smelling her hair? Yes. He was smelling her hair, caging her in his arms, waiting for an answer to his question.

She turned around (what did she do that for?) and decided to face him. To see exactly what he was asking. The only problem was, his eyes were wide and attentive. Nostrils flared. Breathing forced. And his vision was laser-beamed on her lips. She didn't need to have experience with men to know what this was – chemistry.   Unmistakable,   toe-tingling chemistry.

Gianna cleared her throat. "Um...no. There's nothing else I need. If you take care of the customers, I...can...can get a lot done in the kitchen, so..."

"Right," he said, then licked his lips. "But first, there's something I need."

She was afraid to ask, but—

"What's that?" she asked anyway, still caged in muscles. His aura. His smell. *Oh my goodness...*

"I need to put my lips somewhere on you."

"What?"

"I need to put my lips on you."

"Ramsey,   are   you..."   she   grinned uncomfortably. "Are you thinking out loud?"

"No. I know exactly what I'm saying," he told her with heat stirring in his eyes.

Before she could talk him out of it or find a way to escape, he lowered his mouth to her temple and left a simple kiss there. A temple kiss. One in which he knew she could handle. One that wouldn't cause her to spaz out and straight lose it. Granted, he'd loved nothing more than to devour her mouth in a way he'd never done to a woman before, but she couldn't handle that at the moment. He'd have to take his time, get her comfortable with him first, then he'd take off the training wheels and gobble her up.

Looking at her now, he saw her eyes were closed, but like a ray of sun shining brightly after a passing cloud, they opened. And she was looking at him like he was a pot of gold and she was the one who'd just discovered it.

"You...you kissed me," she said, touching her lips, stating the obvious.

"Why are you touching your lips? I didn't kiss those. At least not yet."

Goosebumps ran all down her back, her arms, legs and made her body shiver. "I'm just shocked that you kissed me at all."

His brow raised. "On the temple?"

"Yes."

His lips curved upward. "Yes, I did kiss you on the temple, Gianna, and you better hope that's enough to get me through the rest of the day or I'll be back for more." He reached for the doorknob, finally exiting the office.

She could tell when the smile fell off of his face that he was serious. He *would* be back for more if need be. She chewed on her bottom lip. How would he react when he found out she didn't know the first thing about kissing?

* * *

RAMSEY TOOK CARE of the customers and worked the register like he said he would while Gianna fulfilled catering orders. She had gotten three additional orders throughout the day – a dozen lemon, two dozen strawberry shortcakes and five dozen butter pecan. At the end of the

TINA MARTIN

day, she was exhausted, yet grateful that Ramsey had been there to help her, especially since this rainy day ended up being one of her busiest.

"You sold out of the milk," Ramsey said. Earlier, he moved the refrigerator behind the counter as Gianna had suggested.

"Already?" she asked, looking up at him from her desk.

"Yes. I'm going to have more brought in tomorrow. As for closing duties, I've already swept and mopped the front, turned off the 'Open' sign and wiped down the counter."

"Thank you, Ramsey. I'll take care of the rest. And don't bother ordering more milk. I'll take care of that, too." Gianna typed a note on her computer.

"What more do you have to do before leaving?" he asked.

"Not much."

"Tell me, Gianna."

"I have to mop the kitchen floor, of course, and check the bathroom—"

"I cleaned the bathroom already."

"Ramsey, you don't have to do everything."

"I will if I have to because I'm not leaving here without you."

"Why not? I do this every day except for Sunday. Bake, clean, close up, go home. That's my routine."

"Yeah, well you're not doing this alone tonight."

And she didn't. He was right there to help her sweep the kitchen and mop, take out the garbage and put everything away before it was time to lock up.

After she locked the rear entrance door, she walked to her car with him falling into stride beside her.

"Do you mind if I follow you home?"

"Do I have a choice in the matter?"

"You do as long as you make the right one."

She smirked. "Okay, Ramsey. You can follow me home."

"Good choice."

Chapter 6

WHEN SHE ARRIVED home, she thanked Harriet for watching Gemma, then hugged her before she left. Ramsey spoke with Harriet to get a brief overview of the day and to find out how Gemma was as he walked her to the car. Then he waved at her as she drove way and went back inside to talk to Gianna. When he didn't see her immediately upon entering the house, he headed in the direction of Gemma's bedroom. Of course she'd be there, checking on her little sister. And she was, stooping down beside Gemma's bed, looking at her. Gemma was asleep.

"Goodnight, Gem," she whispered, then stood up. She turned around and saw Ramsey standing at the door. As she approached, he backed out into the hallway, giving her clearance to close the door.

"Talk to me," he said.

"About what?"

"Today was Gemma's first day with Harriet. How do you feel about it?"

Gianna shrugged, walking toward the kitchen.

Ramsey was hot on her trail. "Come on, Gianna. Don't brush me off with a shrug. Talk.

Express your feelings."

"I feel guilty," she said, opening the refrigerator, taking out two bottles of water, handing him one.

"Why?"

She took a swig of water. "Because *I* should be taking care of Gemma."

"That's what you're doing...just with a little help," Ramsey said, twisting the cap off of his water bottle. "For the little while I've known you, I recognize you're one of those people who find it difficult to accept help."

"You're the exact same way. I think all business owners are."

"I have plenty of help, Gianna. I have employees who've helped St. Claire Architects become the brand that it is today. Yeah, I started the company, but I can't take credit for every contract, every bid, every win we've scored. I have a team. I have my brothers. You don't have a team—well, before you met me, you didn't have a team—now you do. I'm team Gianna, and I'll make sure you have enough players on your team to play this game. Harriet is just the beginning."

"I know I've thanked you a thousand times, but once again, thank you for everything, Ramsey. I don't think I would've survived today without you."

"You're welcome." He finished drinking the water then said, "I know how early you go to bed, so I'm going to get out of your hair now. Call me if you need me."

"Okay."

"And I'll be by the bakery at some point tomorrow. I'm going to swing by my office in the morning."

"Trying to catch people not doing their jobs, huh?"

"You know what they say...when the cat's away the mice will play, and by mice, I mean my brothers."

She giggled. "Really?"

"Nah, I'm kidding. I have to make an appearance since I got a call from Regal earlier today. Seems he's run into a roadblock with one of our projects."

"Oh."

"My brothers work as hard as I do. Our father instilled a strong work ethic in each one of us."

"I know he's proud of you and your accomplishments."

"He is, and my mother is, too. She'd be even prouder if one of us settles down and have her some grandbabies."

Gianna's eyebrows raised. "None of your brothers are married?"

"Nope."

"Why not?"

"I guess they haven't found the one. Mother seems to think it's because of me. She thinks if I marry, they'll follow in my footsteps. The sad part is, she's probably right."

"Why is that sad?"

"Well, maybe sad is the wrong choice of word. What I mean is, my relationship status shouldn't determine how my brothers want to live their lives. If they meet that someone special and want to get married, they should by all means get married. Simple as that. Right, Cupcake?"

Gianna hid a smirk.

"I should go now. I'll see you at some point tomorrow."

"Please go handle your business at work. I'll be fine at the bakery. I've become good at multitasking."

He looked at her and could only smile, thinking of all the hard work she put in today with so many catering orders. She was good at handling different tasks at once, but that didn't mean he liked her doing it.

"Goodnight, Gianna." He extended his hand toward her for a shake.

She grasped his hand and shook it just slightly. "Goodnight, Ramsey."

Reluctantly, he let go of her hand and proceeded to the front door. He turned the knob and said, "The milk delivery will be around ten. It's been prepaid already so you shouldn't have a problem there. I explained to them you only needed two crates. That's all the display refrigerator can hold."

"Didn't I tell you not to do that?" she asked, stepping outside with him, standing on the porch.

"Yeah." He smirked. "You did."

Smiling, she shook her head wordlessly.

"And remember to change the cupcake of the day on the chalkboard."

"I will."

"And don't forget to turn on the *open* sign on in the front window."

She smiled. "Will do."

"And one more thing..."

"What's that?"

"Remember to stay sweet."

She blushed, smiling harder, watching as he walked to his Range. Then she stepped back inside and locked the door. She leaned against it and sighed. After a busy, successful day at the bakery, she looked forward to working again tomorrow. The simple improvements Ramsey had made proved to be changes for the better and better operations meant more money. More money meant more funds she'd have to pay for Gemma's medical bills.

Chapter 7

RAMSEY DRESSED IN a black suit. Black shirt. Black Italian leather shoes and a burgundy tie. The platinum cuff links that fastened his shirt sleeves along with the Cartier watch on his left wrist was enough for a down payment on a mansion. He didn't know how long he would have to be in the office today, but he never dressed casually when he had to be there. Work attire meant business. Casual was for play – outside of work – and he took his work too seriously to be stepping up in there with a pair of jeans on.

He took the elevator up to the tenth floor and walked down the hallway toward his office. When he came to his secretary's office, he ducked his head in and said, "Good morning, Judy."

"Good morning, Mr. St. Claire. I didn't know you would be in the office today."

"If it's any consolation, I didn't either. It's all last minute."

"Is there anything I can get for you? Coffee? Water?"

"A cup of coffee would be nice. Also, will you let Regal know I'm here?"

"Will do."

Ramsey continued to his office where he sat at his desk and decided to power on his computer to check emails while he waited for Regal to join him. A few minutes later, Judy was there, placing a cup of coffee on his desk in a tall black mug with the company's logo on it.

Ramsey picked it up, took a sip and said, "Ah, liquid gold. Thank you, Judy."

"You're welcome, Sir. I've already informed Regal that you were here."

Just as she said the words, Regal came walking in along with Romulus and Royal. They were all suited up and rocked serious expressions on their faces.

Ramsey uttered displeasure under his breath. If all three of his brothers were joining him, there was a problem. A big problem. He wasn't ready to deal with this type of problem. Besides, he wasn't even supposed to be here. He wanted to be at the bakery. With Gianna.

Judy closed the door as she left the office and the brothers took seats wherever they deemed most comfortable. Regal sat on the black, leather sofa. Royal perched up on the edge of a conference table using one of the chairs as a placeholder for his feet. Romulus sat in a high back chair – one of two that faced Ramsey's desk.

Biting back frustration, Ramsey asked, "To what do I owe the visit of all three of my brothers?"

Regal spoke up saying, "We need to discuss the new Uptown tower project."

Ramsey frowned. "Why? We submitted the

design and received approval two months ago."

"Correct. However, the city has come back and said that the tower is only approved to be twenty floors high in the location where we want it."

"Five blocks south of the Westin," Ramsey said.

"That's correct," Romulus acknowledged.

Regal added, "If you recall, our client, The Davenport Group, had us design the tower to be thirty floors high."

"Oh, I recall. I did the drawing by hand," Ramsey said. "And I'm sure the city has notified Davenport of this new twenty-floor nonsense."

"Yep," Romulus said. "Dan Davenport requested a meeting with us Friday morning."

Ramsey clenched his teeth. He didn't have time for this – not when he was supposed to be off work. But, he also had a duty to satisfy his clients. After all, The Davenport Group had paid him a lot of money to design the tower.

"The way I see it is, we have two options," Regal said. "We can try to convince Dan to go with the twenty-floor tower if he wants the area near the Westin, or we could keep the thirty floors only if we can find a suitable, comparable location—one that would be approved for a thirty-floor structure."

"Rom, what are our options as far as available space?" Ramsey asked.

"I found an area located near The View high-rise apartments."

"Are you sure that location will be approved

for thirty floors?"

"Yep. They approved a thirty-*five* story building there six months ago, but the developers backed out."

"So, thirty floors shouldn't be a problem if they were willing to approve thirty-five," Regal said, talking it through.

Romulus nodded. "That's what I'm thinking."

Ramsey steepled his hands, strategizing in his head. "Okay...here's what I want to happen. Let's meet Dan and his team Friday afternoon. I'll have Judy make the arrangements—"

"He requested Friday morning," Romulus interjected to say.

"Well, he's not going to get Friday morning," Ramsey said firmly. "We need some time to look into this problem. Meeting him Friday afternoon will give us Friday morning in addition to all day today to get a handle on this situation. Before the meeting occurs, Romulus, I need you to locate two other properties besides the one you currently have for backup."

"Already on it," Romulus responded.

"Regal—I need you to open the blueprint for latest version of the tower, copy it, then revise it to twenty floors and save a copy."

"Easier said than done, but I've already started on it," Regal told him. "A few more hours and it will be complete."

"That's perfect. Send me a copy when you're done," Ramsey instructed. "Royal, I need you to do some digging. Find out why the area by the Westin is no longer zoned for thirty floors and look into the new property Romulus found to determine if thirty floors would present a problem there. And I'm curious...find out why the other developers backed out."

"Got it," Royal said.

"It goes without saying that this all needs to be done by noon tomorrow."

"Yep," Regal said.

"Are we all in accordance?" Ramsey asked.

"We got it," Royal said.

Romulus nodded, then asked, "So, Ram, what have you been doing with all your free time?"

"Yeah, what have you been doing besides dropping in on Ralph and Gilbert, giving them grief?" Royal asked.

"I wouldn't have to drop in on them if I felt like the project was being handled appropriately," Ramsey responded.

"Man, those guys have overseen hundreds of projects for us," Royal said.

"Yeah, and people tend to get comfortable when they've been in a certain position for a long time. I don't want any workers getting comfortable on the job."

"They're hardworking men, Ram," Royal said. "You can't blame *them* if a contractor backs out."

Ramsey sighed. "You're right. You're absolutely right, Royal." Ramsey leaned back in his chair. Then he said, "I met someone."

Romulus frowned. "You met someone? That Wedded Bliss crap actually worked?"

"Well, not necessarily. The woman I'm

interested in just so happens to be the owner's best friend."

Romulus chuckled. "You go straight to the top of the food chain to get yours, huh Ram? I ain't mad at you, bro."

Regal smirked.

"What now? Are you going to marry her?" Royal asked.

"Maybe. If everything goes according to plan."

"I don't think it's a good idea, Ram," Romulus said. "Marrying someone for companionship and not love sounds like a recipe for disaster to me."

Regal had expressed similar concerns.

"Well, what other options do I have? I've lived the single, bachelor lifestyle for over ten years. At some point in life, you have to think about your future—and not just with working and making money. You think about your personal life. About a family and kids and since my heart is closed to love, this is the best option there is."

"Wait...didn't you tell me you haven't felt this way about a woman since Leandra?" Regal asked.

The brothers stared at him in shock.

Ramsey stroked his mustache. "Yes, but it's the feeling. That's all."

Romulus frowned. "What feeling? Don't tell me you're talking about that weird connection crap again."

"That's exactly what I'm talking about. You should know it better than anyone, Rom. You and Siderra have been best friends for years. Since college."

"Yeah," Romulus said. "Friends."

"A friend that you have a close connection to. She practically lives at your house, but that's a discussion for another time. All I'm saying is, something connected me to Gianna the same way it connected me to Leandra. It's a feeling I've only had twice in my life. The first time was with Leandra. I'm experiencing it a second time now."

"But you still don't think you can actually fall in love with her?" Regal asked.

"No, but I do feel something. I like being around her."

"And what if this girl—"

Ramsey cut Romulus off and said, "Not girl. Woman and her name is, Gianna."

"Okay," Romulus continued, "What if *Gianna* falls for you? Then what? You're going to tell her you're incapable of falling in love with her? I don't think that will go over too well with a woman. In fact, I *know* it won't go over well. Does she even know about Leandra?"

"She knows a little, and I doubt she'll fall in love with me. She not looking for love, she's never been in love and she knows nothing about relationships. That much, I know for sure."

"Are you even attracted to her?" Regal asked.

"That's beside the point. You know I've never been one for looks."

"Yet, Leandra was stunning," Romulus

commented.

"Yes, she was," Ramsey said, reflecting, "But we're not talking about her."

"Okay, so what about Gianna, then?" Royal asked. "Is she a looker?"

"Gianna is Gianna. That's all you need to know. You have some major growing up to do if the only thing you find attractive and appealing about a woman is her looks."

"Ay," Royal said, palms up. "All I'm saying is, if I was going to pay for a marriage hookup service, I would at least make sure the woman was a ten. But hey, that's just me I guess."

Ramsey envisioned Gianna's smile and the image of her standing at her front door waving to him last night. The way she wore that hip-hugging dress when she walked in Luce, turning heads on her way to their table, her hair bouncing around her shoulders. He'd let his brothers think what they wanted to think. He knew just how beautiful Gianna was – inside and out. But it was the inside – her heart – that mattered to him the most.

* * *

LATER THAT AFTERNOON, Ramsey walked into the bakery to see that almost all the tables were filled. He glanced at the chalkboard noticing the cupcake of the day was the banana buttercream – and he looked at the display fridge and saw a good supply of milk that would probably be depleted by closing.

When she came walking from the back with

her hairnet and apron, she smiled brightly and said, "Look at you...coming up in here in your three-piece suit, turning heads...got these women salivating and whatnot."

He grinned. "I'm sure it's those banana buttercreams making them salivate."

She giggled. "Would you like to try one?"

"Definitely."

She walked to the display case and removed one, then handed it to him, watching him peel back the liner to take a bite.

After chewing it, he said, "Wow. I think I have a new favorite."

"Oh, yeah?"

"Yes." He took another bite. And within the minute, he'd eaten the whole thing. "How many of these did you bake?"

"Ten dozen. I have about two dozen left."

Walking behind the counter, he asked, "Did you have any catering orders today?"

"Yes. Five. I'm waiting for the last order to be picked up. A woman ordered five dozen vanilla cupcakes with chocolate icing for a party. She said she would be here around four."

"That's awesome."

Gianna walked to the kitchen and removed a dozen carrot cupcakes from the oven. "I made a dozen more carrot cupcakes to last until closing. I think I have enough variety to stop baking for now."

"Alright. Let me jump in here," Ramsey said, rubbing his hands together. "What can I do?"

"Ramsey, you're suited up, and trust me when I say, a black suit like that does not belong around all this flour."

"I have maybe five more identical to this one. If I destroy it, trust me...I won't miss it." He took off his suit jacket, popped off his cuff links, then rolled up his sleeves. "How about I wash some dishes?"

"O-okay. I'm going to go back to the front for a moment."

Gianna stood behind the counter again and sold a few more cupcakes. Shortly after she did, the woman showed up for her cupcake order.

Slowly, the place cleared out. She had her last customer at 6:45 p.m., and immediately after they left, she locked the door. She tallied up the money in the register while Ramsey swept the front dining area.

She looked up and watched him sweep for a moment before saying, "Hey, I packed up some of the leftover banana buttercreams for you."

"Good. It'll be my motivation for working out when I get home."

"You work out?" she asked, then tried to clean it up by saying, "I mean, it's obvious you work out...I was just...never mind." She shook head, baffled at how nerve-racking it was to talk to him.

"Just take your time and ask me what you wanted to ask me."

"I was *trying* to ask if you work out at home."

"I do. I turned one of my sunrooms into a gym."

"You have more than one sunroom?"

"Yes. I have three, actually, well, four if you

consider the floor-to-ceiling wall of windows in my bedroom that faces the lake. One sunroom is a gym, one is a living room type space, and the other is an actual sunroom. They all provide magnificent views of the lake."

"Sounds nice."

"It is. You'll get to see it one day."

Right...sure I will.

He swept trash in the dust pan. "Hey, when was the last time you saw Jerry?"

"He hasn't been in here in a while. I hope nothing happened to him."

Ramsey was thinking about the last time he saw Jerry. They were in the restaurant – at Boardwalk Billy's – and the man had done a disappearing act on him.

"I have a good amount of cupcakes leftover, so I'll be going by the shelter tonight. Do you think Harriet would like some?"

"A couple, maybe." He walked the nearest garbage can and emptied the dust pan. "How's Gemma?"

"She's okay. Harriet said she slept a lot today. I hope she's awake when I get home so I can talk to her for a few minutes."

"Then why don't you go ahead and go," he told her. "I'll lock up here."

"There's no way I'm going to let you lock up alone. You've seriously done enough for me, Ramsey."

"Then let's move faster so we leave together."

"Okay."

* * *

THEY LEFT THE bakery fifteen minutes later, and he followed her to the shelter, then home. She knew what the outcome would be if she told him that following her home was unnecessary, so she didn't bother. One thing she knew about Ramsey was, he was going to do what he wanted to do.

At home, Gianna found Gemma sitting at the kitchen table with Harriet. She rushed over to her, leaned down and wrapped her arms around her, pressing her lips to Gemma's cheek.

"Somebody's happy to see me," Gemma teased.

"I am happy to see you," Gianna said, excited, full of love. "When I got home yesterday, you were asleep. I didn't get to talk to you. How do you feel?"

Gemma grinned. "Sleepy."

"Well, besides that."

"I've been sick for so long, I don't know how I feel anymore."

Gianna glanced at Harriet.

"She ate pretty good," Harriet said. "And we watched a little TV."

"Good." Gianna handed Harriet a small box as she stood straight up again. "I brought you some cupcakes, Harriet."

"Oh. Thank you, darling," Harriet said, looking at the sweet treats.

"They're banana buttercream," Ramsey said, stepping inside the kitchen after ending a phone call with Romulus.

"I can't wait to try them," Harriet said.

"Don't do it," Gemma told her. "Once you do, you're hooked."

Gianna giggled.

"Is that so?" Harriet asked.

"Yes. That's so," Ramsey said. "She's already got me hooked." *Got me hooked on more than just her cupcakes.* He glanced at Gianna and smiled. If only she knew what he was thinking.

"Well, I'm going to get on the road so I can get a good night's rest and be back here bright and early tomorrow," Harriet said.

"Harriet, where do you live?" Gianna asked.

"In the Northlake Mall area."

"Oh, so you're not all that far away."

"Not at all."

"I'll see you tomorrow, Mrs. Harriet," Gemma said.

"Yes. Get your rest, sweetie. We're going to have a lil' fun tomorrow."

"Okay. Rest is what I do best," Gemma replied, unenthused.

"Thanks again, Harriet," Gianna said.

"You're welcome, dear."

"I'll walk you out, Harriet," Ramsey offered. He was a gentleman like that, but it would also give him time to get an update on Gemma. Standing by Harriet's car, he asked, "So, how is she?"

Harriet sighed, relieving the weight of taking care of an ill, young woman who had her whole life ahead of her – the world at her fingertips – but cancer put her life on hold. There was nothing fair about these circumstances. Nothing at all. Gemma deserved so much more than the hand she'd been dealt. Shaking her head, Harriet said, "She's not doing all that good. And I don't know why the doctor gave her those pills, Ramsey. They don't seem to be doing a darn thing to help her. The only time she smiles is when we talk about Gianna." Harriet sighed heavily again. "She's such a sweet young lady. It's so hard to watch her go through this."

"Yeah, now imagine how hard it is for Gianna."

"And what about you, Ramsey? I assume this must be difficult for you as well, considering what you've been through in the past."

Ramsey slid his hands in his pockets, glancing down the lighted street, then focused his attention back on Harriet. "It's definitely not easy, but since I've been through this before, I figured I could help her."

"Really?"

"Yes, Harriet. Really."

"A woman you just met?"

"We didn't *just* meet. I've known her for two weeks now." He smirked when he realized two weeks was nothing to brag about considering how hard he was going in for this woman.

"And I bet Bernadette don't know a thing about her."

"No, but she will."

"Well, I agree...if anyone can help Gianna, it would be you, but helping Gianna involves more than just *helping Gianna*. It very much involves the care and well-being of her sister."

Ramsey nodded. He was aware that Gianna's happiness was directly linked to Gemma's health. She practically raised her sister and wanted her to thrive, grow up, fall in love, get married – all that.

"But you don't need an old lady telling you what to do, I'm sure."

"No, Harriet, I appreciate the advice. I'm actually glad you can see how close they are. Gianna adores her sister."

Harriet nodded. "And I have a hunch that you adore Gianna."

Happiness glowed in his eyes. "Your hunch would be correct."

Harriet patted him on the arm. "Let me get on out of here. I'll see you later."

"Drive safe, Harriet."

"I will."

She drove away and Ramsey walked back inside of the house. Now, he could concentrate on his girl. He found Gianna in Gemma's bedroom, hugging her, then helping her settle comfortably underneath the covers.

"Hey, I didn't get my goodnight hug," Ramsey said.

"Okay, bring it in," Gemma said.

Gianna stood back while Ramsey embraced Gemma. Then he stood upright again. He brushed the back of his index finger across the tip of her nose and said, "Goodnight, Gem."

"Goodnight, Ramsey," she said softly with her eyes closed.

Gianna smiled, then she and Ramsey walked out of the room and headed back for the kitchen.

"How about breakfast for dinner tonight?" Gianna asked. "It won't take me long to whip up some breakfast food."

"No. I don't want you to do that. You've already been working hard today."

"I don't mind. I've been working hard my whole life. Now, how do you like your eggs?"

He hesitated to answer. He really didn't want her to cook after she'd been standing on her feet all day baking. But he watched her take a frying pan from the bottom drawer of the stove. Then she removed eggs, cheese and bacon from the refrigerator. "Do you have a preference?" she asked.

"No," he said reluctantly.

Gianna mixed the eggs in a bowl, cut up cheddar cheese then fried strips of bacon. She cooked the cheesy eggs last and made two whole wheat, buttered toasts. She served him a plate then sat down with her own.

"Thank you, Gianna."

She glanced up. "You're welcome, Ramsey."

She took a fork full of eggs to her mouth and said, "I really didn't expect you to come to the bakery today."

"Why not?"

"Because of your work emergency."

He watched her for a moment, his own mouth watering at the sight of her biting into a strip of bacon. "What makes you think it was an emergency?"

"I just assumed it was."

"Why?" he asked, sitting up taller, anticipating her answer.

She smiled nervously. "Well, you said you'd taken a month off of work. I knew you wouldn't go back into the office if the situation wasn't an urgent one. I could be wrong though. I'll admit...I'm not all that good at reading people."

"You're right. It was an emergency of sorts."

"What happened?"

When he finished chewing the fork full of eggs he'd taken to his mouth a moment ago, he said, "We ran into an issue with one of our designs."

"What kind of issue?" she inquired.

"A zoning problem. Seems Charlotte doesn't want a particular tower we designed built close to an Uptown hotel unless it's twenty floors. The developers wanted thirty floors."

"Oh," Gianna said realizing the extent of his dilemma. "I don't know the ins and outs of it, but it sounds like a pain."

"It is, but we'll get through it. It wouldn't be the first time we've run into issues with plans and developers and city officials. It's a never-ending battle. Trust me."

"So, how do you fix it?"

"Well, we had to come up with plans 'B' and 'C' to present to the developers tomorrow afternoon."

"You don't seem stressed out about it at all."

"I'm not. My brothers are handling most of the leg work. My job is to sell it to the developers, and that won't be easy. People want what they want…nothing less. More maybe, but definitely not less."

Gianna nodded.

Ramsey finished the last of his food and thought now was a good time to ask her a question he wanted to ask yesterday. Felicity would be meeting with her in the morning and he wanted her as conditioned as possible. "Gianna?"

She glanced up briefly but not long enough for their eyes to connect and hold.

"What do you think about me?" he asked.

"As a person?"

"Yes."

"I think you're a decent person. Kind. Caring. Of course, I realize it could all be a scam."

He chuckled. "A scam?"

Smiling, she said, "Yes. When people meet, oftentimes they show the very best of themselves. Put their best foot forward. Then, further down the road, you see the worst—the red flags—the big, ugly foot."

"Wow."

"It's true."

"So, I'm one big red flag waiting to happen."

"No, that's not what—"

"You should learn to focus on the good in people, Gianna—not the bad," he said.

"I *do* focus on the good."

"How, when you, in one breath, said I was a kind *scammer*? How do you even use the words *kind* and *scammer* in the same sentence?"

She giggled. "Okay. I apologize. I don't think you're a scammer. You're generous—too generous for me, and I honestly feel that you've given me more than what I deserve."

"That's not your call to make," he said standing, walking over to the refrigerator to get water. He handed her a bottle and sat down again.

"Here's what I don't get," she said. "If you are really the way you present yourself to me, why aren't you taken by now?"

He was glad she asked that question. It would give him an opportunity to explain his position – a crucial point she needed to know before meeting with Felicity. "Remember when I told you about my last relationship...my fiancée, who passed away?"

"Yes."

"That was fifteen years ago, and I haven't loved a woman since. Five years after Leandra passed, my mother begged me to go to therapy, and I did just to appease her, but it didn't fix me. I could date a woman but never develop feelings for her. The therapist told me I was broken."

Gianna frowned, "What does that mean?"

"She explained that it was normal for me to experience a broken heart after losing Leandra, but she said I never rebounded, and I probably never would."

"That's awful," Gianna said, frowning. She couldn't imagine being with a man who couldn't love her.

"Is it?" he asked.

"Yes. Everyone deserves love."

"This coming from the woman who told me she didn't have time for love."

"I don't, but I didn't close my heart off to it. That's what it sounds like you've done."

"Maybe, but you wanted to know why I wasn't taken. That's why."

"Right," she said, then took a sip of water. "Now I see why you have all the time in the world to take on a charity case."

His brows furrowed. "You're referring to yourself as a charity case?"

"Well, yeah. You've done things for me that I wasn't financially able to do for myself."

"That doesn't make you a charity case. You own your own bakery, Gianna. You should be proud."

A small smile touched her lips. She should have been proud, and she was in the beginning, but then Gemma got sick and her passion became work. Something she loved to do became something she *had* to do.

"Tomorrow, I'm not sure if I'll be able to stop by the bakery," he told her.

"That's fine. My friend Felicity is coming by in the morning...said she had to talk to me about something."

Ramsey knew what that *something* was. He turned up the bottle of water to his mouth. "Thanks for cooking. The food was delicious."

"It was?"

"Yes. It was."

"Sorry I couldn't prepare something a little more dinnerly."

"Dinnerly?" He chuckled. "You know that's not a word, right?"

"But you know what I mean, don't you?"

"Yes." He laughed. "I know exactly what you mean, but don't worry about it. This meal was perfect."

"I know you're just trying to make me feel better."

"No, I really do appreciate it. You didn't have to cook anything, but you did. Thank you."

She smiled. "You're welcome."

Ramsey yawned, stretching his arms up in the air. "I know you're ready to kick me out so you can go to bed, but I'm not ready yet."

"Well, since Gemma is all taken care of, I have an hour or so to entertain you. Would you like to go sit in the living room and watch TV or something?"

"Sure," he said, standing, following her lead. She sat on the couch, leaning forward to take the remote from the coffee table then powered on the TV.

Ramsey sat next to her, angling his body in her direction. He took the remote out of her grasp, powered the TV off and said, "On second thought, let's just talk. Me and you. No TV."

Gianna tried to conceal her nervousness, tried to pretend the warmth from his hand hadn't sparked a flame that made her suddenly crave a bottle of thirst-quenching water. "Talk about what?"

He shrugged. "Whatever. We talk a lot about you. Why don't you ask me something?"

"Oh. Okay. Um...okay. Tell me about your brothers. I know we talked about them before...how none of them are married. So, um...what do they do for a living?"

"They all work for St. Claire Architects. I'm pretty sure I told you that, too."

"You probably did." *I'm just a nervous wreck right now.*

"Regal is an architect as well. We actually graduated college together."

"How old is he?"

"He's thirty-five. Then there's Romulus. He's thirty. He's our land finder. And Royal, the youngest, is the troubleshooter. Any issues that prohibit the progress of a project funnels through him."

"And how old is he?"

"Twenty-five."

"Awesome. I like how you all are spaced apart in age."

"I'm sure it wasn't planned. In fact, my mother will tell you the only reason Romulus, Regal and Royal are here is because she wanted a girl...ended up with three knuckleheads instead and never did get that daughter she always wanted."

Gianna laughed.

He watched her intently, studying the dimple in her jaw, the shape of her lips when she laughed and the joy in her eyes.

She looked away from him, trying hard to think of another question to ask. "Um...so any kids?"

"Do *I* have kids?"

"Any of you."

"No," Ramsey answered. "There are no kids."

"None?"

"Zilch," he responded.

"Your brothers don't have girlfriends?"

"No. They date, but I don't think they're looking for any attachments at this point in their lives."

"Right, because of you."

"Not necessarily. I told you that's what my mother thinks, but my brothers have their own strong, individual minds. If they wanted a relationship, they'd have one."

Gianna nodded, glancing at his hand and admiring his well-manicured, clean, even-clipped fingernails. She could tell he was a man who took extreme care of himself. "I have to say, Ramsey...I've never met a guy like you."

"I'll take that as a compliment. Means I'm not ordinary."

"Oh, there's *nothing* ordinary about you. Crap!" She covered her mouth. "I just said that out loud, didn't I?"

He laughed. "Yes, you did, and by the way, there's nothing ordinary about you either, Gianna."

Gianna's eyes flashed amusement. "Like you had to tell me that..."

After the longest minute ever of awkward silence, Ramsey sighed and leaned back, resting his head on the back of the couch.

"I know you're exhausted, Ramsey."

"I am, and I still have to workout when I get

home."

"Seriously? After everything you've done today?"

"Yes. Exercise relieves stress."

"And what do you have to be stressed out about?"

"You'd be surprised. Everything in my life isn't perfect just because I have money."

"Okay, so what do you have to be stressed about then?" she asked again.

Still leaned back, he adjusted his position so he could look at her. He casually lowered his hand to her knee and responded, "Well, I got that issue I'm handling at work tomorrow."

"Right."

"And then, my girlfriend is stressed out because she has so much on her plate and her sister is sick, so I worry about her constantly," he said palming her knee.

Gianna's eyes twinkled. He just referred to her as his girlfriend. Maybe he was just joking though. She couldn't tell. "What else?"

"Oh, you're just going to skip right over the girlfriend comment, huh?"

Gianna smiled.

And he smiled too, flashing a relaxed, laid back smile that made her want to scoot closer to him and feel comfortable in his arms. But she didn't. "I heard the comment. I just—I've never been anyone's girlfriend."

You've never been anyone's wife either but I want you to be mine. Girlfriend doesn't make you mine, but a marriage license does. You moving into my home does. You letting your guard down with me, wearing the beautiful ring I'm going to pick out for you and trusting me with your life does.

And then his hand moved from her knee to her thigh and she jumped.

He didn't like that. Well, he did like it but he wasn't okay with her still not being comfortable with him. Felicity was due to drop a bombshell on her tomorrow about his proposal and if she wasn't comfortable enough, she probably wouldn't accept it. That bothered him because she couldn't say no. She just couldn't. He needed her to be that missing puzzle piece in his life. There's no way he could walk away now.

He stood up.

"Are you leaving?" she asked.

"Yes. I should go."

"Why so soon?"

"I have to prepare for tomorrow." *In more ways than one.*

Gianna stood up and walked with him to the front door.

"Maybe I'll see you on Saturday," he said, extending his hand to her. He wanted to grab the woman, pull her in to him – hold her right up against his body and never let go. Instead, he had to settle for a measly handshake.

Gianna reached for his hand.

He clutched hers, squeezed it firmly as if they were closing an important business deal.

By the way he gripped her hand with a firm amount of pressure, it only made her turn to mush. And his eyes...they were gradually getting darker she noticed. She caught herself from falling into the deep abyss of his soul.

"Are you okay?" he asked, slowly releasing her hand.

"Yes. I'm fine."

"Okay. Goodnight, Gianna."

"Goodnight, Ramsey," she responded.

He released her hand slowly, then walked away, wondering if this would be the last time, the last visit, the last interaction he would have with this special, quirky, refreshingly awesome woman. After her meeting with Felicity, she would probably think he was a flake and avoid him like the plague. He hoped for the opposite reaction, because he was a man who knew what he wanted, and even though that didn't include love, it did include Gianna Jacobsen.

Chapter 8

"HEY, FELICITY!" GIANNA said darting from behind the counter to greet Felicity with an all-encompassing bear hug. "Long time, no see," she said, squeezing harder.

"Girl it ain't been that long. I do need to breathe."

Gianna released her. "You look good. I love the whole ensemble," she said, her eyes rolling down to Felicity's black heels, black pencil skirt and fun, flirty red wine-colored blouse.

"Thanks. Now, where's my cupcake?"

"Do you want the chocolate fudge?"

"You know it. Hey, by the way, I'm diggin' the updates you've made around here. The chalkboard looks awesome. Ooh, lookey...you even drew a cute little cupcake on there."

"Well, I can't take the credit for that."

And Felicity had an idea why...

Gianna came back to the table with two coffees – regular for Felicity, decaf for herself. Then she walked back to the showcase to get a chocolate fudge cupcake. She placed it next to Felicity's coffee cup.

"Looks delish." Felicity sipped coffee.

"So, what's up?" Gianna asked. "I see you got your binder, looking all official and whatnot."

Felicity grinned. "Well, I had to come with

my binder because well, this is sort of a business visit."

Gianna tilted her head. "A business visit? With me?"

"Okay, let me explain. Do you remember me mentioning a problem client I had?"

"The most recent problem client. Yeah. You said something about him refusing to look at the matches you sent to him or something."

"Yes. That's the one."

"Okay. What about him?" Gianna took a sip of coffee.

"So, since I wasn't doing a good job, apparently, of matching him with someone, he asked me if he could browse through the website and find his own potential matches. You know me...I told him to go for it because I was already fed up at that point, and I was sure he'd come running back for my help eventually, but he didn't. He walked into my office with an arrogant stride and brought me the profile of the woman he said he wanted."

Felicity removed the sheet of paper from the pocket of her binder, then placed it on the table in front of Gianna. She bit into her cupcake watching Gianna's face scrunch up as her eyes scanned the profile.

"This—this is my information," Gianna said in shock, looking up at Felicity.

"It is. Remember you added it for me when we were testing out the system?"

"Yes, but you inactivated it."

"No, I *thought* I inactivated your profile. I didn't. Even still, it's surprising that someone even looked at it being you didn't have a profile picture. Profiles without pictures usually get skipped."

"Okay, so what now?" Gianna took another sip of coffee.

"Aren't you the least bit curious to know who the guy is?" Felicity asked her.

"Doesn't matter. I'm not being *set up* with anyone and I'm definitely not marrying some dude I don't know, so you can tell whoever it is that it's not going to happen."

Felicity narrowed her eyes at her friend. "Why not?"

"Because it's not, Felicity."

"Because you're afraid to try new things. Live a little."

"No. Because I have better things to do with my time than trying to please a man."

Felicity giggled. If she only knew who the man was...

"What's so funny?"

"I'm curious about something. Remember the guy you went out on that date with? You *should* remember because it's the only date you've ever been on and you described it as a complete disaster."

"Yes, I remember."

"What was his name? You told me about the date, but you never mentioned the guy's name."

"His name is Ramsey," Gianna answered. "But how's that relevant to—"

"Last name, St. Claire?" Felicity interrupted to ask and couldn't drop the grin from her face as she watched Gianna's eyes brighten.

"Yes. How'd you know that?"

"*He's* the guy, Gianna. My problem client—the man who brought me your profile. He wants you."

Gianna grinned a little before actual, real laughter erupted. She laughed so hard, tears came to her eyes. This had to be a joke. It had to be, but though amused, Felicity wasn't laughing.

When her laughter subsided, she looked at Felicity and asked, "What are you trying to do right now because this is funny. Well, not really all *that* funny, but still..." she said, still tickled.

"I'm not joking, Gianna. Tall, dark, and extremely fine, Ramsey St. Claire walked into my office with this piece of paper and said he wanted to put a ring on it."

All traces of humor went away from her face. "Wait...you're serious?"

"Yeah!" Felicity said, brightening her eyes. "I am. So, what are you going to do about it?"

"B-b-but this can't be. Why would he want to marry me?"

Felicity shrugged. "He said he was attracted to what a person was on the inside and didn't pay that much attention to the outside which is probably why he didn't want women with implants and fake...well, fake everything."

"Huh?"

Felicity explained, "During one of our meetings, he told me he didn't want a lot of fakeness. He said he wanted a true, genuine, down-to-earth woman."

"So, in other words, he thinks I'm ugly."

"No. That's not what that means. And why didn't you tell me *he* was the guy you went out with?"

"How was I supposed to know that you two actually knew each other, Felicity? I didn't know Ramsey was a client of yours. He never told me anything about joining Wedded Bliss."

"Skip what he didn't tell you. I want to know about all this stuff you didn't tell me. Like the fact that he SPENT THE NIGHT WITH YOU!"

Gianna hid her face behind her hands. "I can explain."

"Please do you lil' thot...trying to play the innocent role and got this man all up and through your crib and God only knows what else he done been all up in."

She eased her hands down on the table and looked at Felicity, rocking a smile on her face. "Get your mind out of the gutter, Felicity. It was nothing like that. What happened was, I was in the grocery store trying to buy some food and my credit card declined. Ramsey was there, too—he wasn't with me, he just happened to be there—and he paid for my food, followed me home and helped me put the groceries away. Then we talked and I fell asleep. According to Gemma, he put me to bed."

Felicity lifted a brow. "Put you to bed how? Like tucked you in, or put you to bed like J. Holiday? With your eyes rolling back in your head and all that?"

Gianna laughed. "You're awful."

"And you didn't answer."

"It was completely innocent, Felicity. I can assure you."

"How did you meet him?"

"He came here, to the bakery two weeks ago, staring me down. No, well he actually startled me while I was on the phone with Gem."

"And you two just hit it off from there?"

"I guess you can say that. He told me straight up that he had a connection with me. Told me I could *use* him any way I saw fit. Said he was my real-life guardian angel."

Felicity quirked up her lips. "He actually told you those things?"

"Yes, and he meant them. He hired a nurse to watch after Gemma while I'm working. All these little updates you see around here—he did them. Now, I'm wondering if this was all a part of his plan to get me to agree to this," she said gesturing towards the profile.

"So, what if it was? Do you like him?"

"Yes. I like him. I told him he was a good person, and I meant it."

"Then marry him. You know the motto for Wedded Bliss...marry today, get to know each other tomorrow. It's the way of the future."

Gianna shook her head.

Felicity continued, "He said he would pay me double if I could see this through. It costs ten grand for my services. He'll pay twenty."

"If I agree to marry him, he's going to pay you twenty thousand dollars?"

"Yes, ma'am."

"This is insane," Gianna said. "And it sucks. I thought he genuinely liked me. I didn't know he had ulterior motives."

"Wait...slow down. Based on my meeting with him, I do think his *like* of you is genuine. And, he's expressed a desire to do more in regards to helping Gemma."

Gianna's stomach balled up in knots. She hugged herself, leaning forward. "I can't believe this is happening to me."

"Hey, it could be a good thing, Gianna."

"Are you kidding me? I have no idea what to do with a man. Besides, Gemma needs me now more than ever and—"

"And you need someone, too. I try to be there as much as I can, Gianna, but I'll admit...it's hit or miss. I'm just as busy as you are these days. This man, for whatever reason, chose you and I think you need to give it some serious thought."

"He told me he was incapable of falling in love, Felicity.

"Then there you have it. You don't want love anyway, right? This is the perfect setup."

"But what if I start having feelings for him? Then what?"

"That's a big if."

"Yes, but it's not totally unfeasible. I don't want to be stuck with a guy who I love and he can't love me back."

"Honestly, I didn't like it when he told me that."

"Told you what?"

"About his inability to love, but to offset that flaw, he told me things he was willing to do for you in exchange for your companionship. He said he'd take care of you. He told me he wanted to get Gemma the highest form of care possible. Said he would pay every outstanding hospital bill Gem has and he would prevent your house from going into foreclosure. Not to mention paying off your car and get this—he even said he would pay the lease on the bakery for the next ten years."

"How does he know—?" She frowned. "Have you been telling him all this personal stuff about me and my finances?"

"No. I was very particular about what I told him. He came at me with this. I thought *you* told him."

"Okay, maybe Gemma told him about the hospital bills, but how does he know about the house, the car and the lease on the—? " She stopped talking and said, "O-M-G...that night he stayed at my house, he probably saw my shoebox of bills."

Felicity snapped her head back. "Your what?"

"I'm old school, I know, but I've been keeping all the bills I can't afford to pay in a shoebox on my dresser."

"You keep your bills in a freakin' shoebox?"

"Yes, but don't lose sight of the more important issue at hand, here. Ramsey must've gone through them! How else would he know I'm behind on this place? And my car. And my bakery. And the house." Gianna covered her face with her hands and said, "Oh my God. This is so embarrassing. He's known all this time."

"Gianna—"

"I mean, if having my card decline three times at the grocery store isn't embarrassing enough, now he knows everything. That I'm broke...on the verge of bankruptcy."

"So what?"

"You can't see how embarrassing this is for me, Felicity? He's this great architect dude and I'm just a wannabe business owner who can't afford to pay her own bills. And I'm supposed to marry him so he can make all of my troubles go away."

"Sounds like a sweet deal to me."

"Felicity!" Gianna stood up and paced the floor. "It's not a sweet deal. It's me admitting that I'm a failure and I need a man to rescue me. It means *he* thinks I'm so desperate, I'd enter into a marriage with a man who could never love me."

"You make it sound so harsh," Felicity said, trying to downplay Gianna's concerns. "Listen, just think about it, Gianna. You don't have to make a decision now. But as a part of your decision-making process, please, please, *puh-leese* take into account that I've only had two successful clients this year and if you agree to this one, it'll be a two-for-one deal since he's paying double. And I'm a good judge of character. You know this."

"Yeah, and you hate him. He's your *problem* client, remember?"

"Well, he was being a jerk to me, but hey, that's me. Maybe our personalities didn't click. It's a totally different story with you. He really was genuine about his request."

"If he's so genuine, why didn't he mention anything about this proposal when I saw him last night?"

"Well, he *did* hire me to find him a match. I suppose he thought it was my job to do so. And look at all the nice things he's already done for you. I think it'll be the perfect arrangement."

"That's the thing, Felicity. I don't know if I'm ready for an *arrangement*. I just want to take care of Gemma. That's all."

"And think about how much better you'll be able to do that with the support of your new hubby bear." Felicity waggled her eyebrows.

"You make it sound so easy."

"It is easy. Sign a few papers and, bada bing bada boom—you're the future Mrs. Gianna St. Claire."

The sound of that twisted her stomach.

"Just think about it," Felicity said, gathering her notebook when a few customers came inside of the bakery. She stood up and said, "Listen...I have to run by the office, but I'll be back around lunch to help you out today."

"Fine, but I won't have an answer by then," Gianna said, then walked behind the counter to greet her customers.

"Good morning. What can I get for you?" she asked the couple and when they responded, she watched their mouths move, but didn't hear a word they said. She could only focus on what Felicity had just told her about Ramsey. What was she going to do now?

Chapter 9

SHE WOULD BE the first to admit that she was naïve, but something about the way she and Ramsey had met seemed legitimate. Now, she was having second thoughts. Maybe he'd planned their initial meeting as precisely and down to the detail like he planned his building designs in hopes of acquiring her. Would he be that methodical and if so why was he plotting this with her?

"This doesn't make any sense," she said softly. "Why would he go to such extreme measures for me?" she asked while stirring baking soda with flour and sugar in a bowl, adding butter, then mixing more. This would be the last batch of blueberry lemon cupcakes for the day. She was glad of that. She couldn't wait to close shop so she could get her head on straight again if that was even possible. Felicity had come there this morning and shook up her entire universe. It still hadn't quite registered.

After preparing the mixture, she filled two cupcake pans and placed them in the oven. Checking the lobby, she saw a few customers still there. She wiped down the counter by the register again and cleaned up at the coffee station. Several times she had to catch her balance. Thinking about the possibility of being with a man like Ramsey had her dizzy. She couldn't be with him. No way! Everything about the proposal Felicity pitched felt wrong, and he was a distraction she didn't need, especially when it came down to where her attention should've been focused – on Gemma.

* * *

RAMSEY – DRESSED IN a dark navy, Armani suit with a crisp white shirt and blue and white diagonal striped tie – left his home in Lake Norman, heading for Charlotte. He had business to attend to today at the office but his mind wasn't on St. Claire Architects or Dan Davenport. It was solely on Gianna. Today, Felicity was to present his proposal and he could about imagine how Gianna would react to it. She'd think he was nuts. In a way, he *had* lost his mind and it was all her fault. Well, not primarily her fault, but he couldn't deny himself of the attraction – the pull he felt to his abdomen every time their eyes connected. He hadn't felt anything remotely close to this in fifteen years.

In a way, it scared him. What if this was infatuation like Regal had claimed? He frowned, made the turn down her street toward her house, heading to see Gemma. With an hour and some change to work with, he had ample time to get to the office to meet with his brothers. But first, he wanted to spend some time with Gemma.

He pulled in the driveway. Seemed weird since Gianna wasn't there but he needed to have a real, open, honest, uninterrupted conversation with Gemma.

Harriet opened the door. "Hey, Ramsey," she said as she did so. "What are you doing here?"

"I need to speak with Gemma," he said as he stepped inside.

"Oh. She's eating her breakfast," Harriet said as she walked to the kitchen.

Ramsey was right behind her, watching Gemma's face light up when she realized he was there.

"Ooh...look at you," she said.

Ramsey could tell she was trying hard to be upbeat – trying to wake herself up even though he could see how tired she was. He turned to Harriet and asked, "Harriet, can you give me a moment with Gemma?

"Sure," Harriet said, leaving the kitchen.

"You look nice," Gemma told him as she stirred her oatmeal.

"Thank you."

"Where are you off to?"

"I have to go by the office. I have an important meeting today," he said, analyzing her. He saw the darkness and chafeness around her eyes. She looked more fragile today for some reason. And when she picked up a spoon to eat, her hands shook.

"I'm going to talk to Gianna about this, but I wanted to discuss it with you first."

"Discuss what?"

"Your health. Your condition isn't improving."

Gemma coughed. "Well, I just started taking the pills on Monday. We have to...have to give them a chance to work."

"While you're giving them a chance, you're letting time pass when you could be starting something else that's guaranteed to work."

"Like what? A miracle of some sort?"

Ramsey grimaced. "No. There are other treatment options your doctor failed to offer you because he knows you can't afford it."

Gemma sighed. "Did Gianna put you up to this?"

"No."

"Then, why are you smiling?"

"Just the mention of Gianna's name makes me smile."

"Seriously?" Gemma smiled beautifully.

"Yes, seriously. Gianna has no idea I'm here."

"Well, listen, Ramsey. I thank you for the positive thinking—" she coughed, "But I can't keep putting my sister through this. I can't keep putting myself through all of this."

"All of what? Trying to get better?"

"Yes."

He frowned. "So your alternative is to give up? Is that it, because if it is, I'm sorry. That's not acceptable."

"Not acceptable for who?"

"For me, for Gianna, and you shouldn't accept it either."

Gemma cleared her throat. "You have no

idea how it feels to be poked and prodded, filled with hope one day and falling down to the lowest level the next."

"You're right. I don't know how it feels to be poked and prodded. I'm in good health. I have no reason to be poked, but I do know how it feels to have hope, only to be let down. I know that all too well. I was engaged, fifteen years ago. She—she died of lung cancer. The woman I loved with all of my heart died. There was nothing I could do then, but there is something I can do for you, Gemma. Gianna loves you. You said it yourself—she'd do anything for you, right?"

Gemma nodded.

"Then don't you think it's time to return the favor? Time to do something for her? It's easy to give up, but in life, you have to fight. Fight with all the love you feel for your sister and try to work with me here, Gem. Now, I've already contacted the nearest cancer treatment center. It's in Georgia. When I get you scheduled, can you commit to going?"

Gemma looked downward.

"Come on, Gem. Do it for Gianna."

"That's the thing...I thought I was doing everything I'm doing for Gianna. I know the doctor is selling me false hopes."

"*That* doctor. Yes. But did you know that surgery can cure lung cancer in some patients?"

"It can?"

"Yes. The doctor didn't mention that to you, huh?"

"No."

"See, that's what I'm talking about. I guarantee you if your doctor knew you had someone who'd be willing to pay hundreds of thousands of dollars, he'd change his tune."

"You'd be willing to do that for—for me?"

"Yes, Gemma. I am not going to stand around and do nothing. It doesn't matter how long you've been convincing yourself that death is the easiest way out...I can't let you die."

Tears came to her weak eyes.

Ramsey reached across the table and held Gemma's fragile hands. "I promised you that I would take care of your sister. The first day I met you, I made that promise to you, remember?"

Gemma nodded.

"A big part of taking care of Gianna is taking care of you. Okay?"

Gemma nodded again.

Ramsey stood up and invited her to stand with him. Carefully, he placed his hand on her head and held her close to him as she cried. "Don't cry, Gemma. Everything's going to be okay now."

Gemma continuously wept in his arms and he consoled her. And while he did so, he recognized the differences between his reaction to Gemma in tears versus his reaction to Gianna. To see any woman cry was hard for him – for any *real* gentleman – but Gemma's tears weren't as nearly as painful to take as Gianna's. Amazing how he had such strong feelings for a woman he'd known less than a month. She grew on him faster than any other woman he'd ever taken a liking to after Leandra died. And there were plenty he had *liked* but never one whom he introduced to his parents. His brothers. Never one he'd invited into his home. Never one he'd give the world for. But for Gianna, he looked forward to doing all these things, and he'd do anything within his power to take care of her and Gemma.

Gemma's cries slowly ceased and he released her, staring down into her eyes. "I'm not going to let you fail, Gemma. You're nineteen. You have so much living to do. Do you know that?"

She smiled through her tears. "If you say so, Ramsey."

"I *do* say so. Now, finish up your breakfast and get some rest, sweetie."

"Okay."

"We'll talk again, soon."

Chapter 10

"I SENT EVERYBODY a revised copy of the Davenport Tower," Regal said.

"I'm looking at it now," Ramsey said staring at the thirty-four-inch curved monitor on his desk. He had the blueprint on the left side of the screen, his uploaded hand sketch of the building on the right and his email inbox opened on the middle screen.

Royal and Romulus were looking at the revised design from their Surface Pro tablets. Ramsey rubbed his chin, thinking. "Regal, remind me what this tower is to be used for again."

"For business offices. My guess would be businesses like insurance companies, banks...the bottom floor will house a few restaurants and shops, similar to The Americas Bank tower on the corner of Trade and Tryon. Do you know what I'm talking about?"

"Yes, I'm familiar," Ramsey responded.

"How many floors does that building have?" Romulus asked.

"Fifty," Regal answered.

"By the way, I confirmed that the location by The View is available and zoned for thirty or more floors," Romulus said. "So, if all else fails, we can use it as an option."

"And I found out why the area near the Westin isn't zoned for thirty floors," Royal chimed in to say. "It's an aesthetics issue. The city believes the area would be better served with a shorter structure in order to keep up the Uptown appeal."

Ramsey looked up at his brother. "Please tell me you're joking."

"I wish I was, bruh, but that was their exact words. Caught me off guard."

"We could fight them on that," Regal said. "It's nonsense. I guarantee you, if we walk away from that site, there will be a tower being constructed there in less than a year."

"No doubt about it," Romulus said.

"What do you suggest we do, Royal?" Ramsey asked looking at his brother.

Royal looked surprised. "You're asking me?"

"Yes. I'm asking you."

"In that case, I suggest we proceed with our plans for thirty floors—"

"Even though we can't get zoned for thirty?" Ramsey asked.

Regal glanced at Ramsey. He knew Ramsey was testing Royal. Ramsey had an issue with Royal thinking he was in charge. Since he wanted to parlay like he had some authority, Ramsey was testing him to see if he would've made the same decision as he would have regarding this particular matter.

"Yes. We should move forward," Royal said a second time, confirming his conviction. "I'm sure the city has tried this tactic with other businesses as well in order to keep certain areas vacant for new construction that *they* want in the area. This is unacceptable and I think we should give them a little heat. In the meantime, it would be wise to lay out all our cards with Dan so he knows what we're working on and what the possible hiccups may be. Who knows, he may decide to pull the project from the old location and request a different area—to which Romulus has already found a suitable backup."

All eyes went back to Ramsey. "Good call, Royal. Let's go into the meeting with Dan with Royal's plan and we'll take it from there."

Royal's brows raised. "Seriously?"

"Yes," Ramsey answered. "Seriously."

"You're actually going with *my* plan?" Royal asked. Like his other brothers, he couldn't believe it either.

Ramsey smirked. "Yes, Royal. I'm going with your plan."

"What's the catch?" Royal asked, narrowing his eyes. Ramsey never went with his plan. Why the sudden strategic shift? Did he think his plan was garbage and wanted to see him fail, or did he legitimately believe he'd presented a good idea?

"There is no catch, Royal. I realize we've been clashing a lot lately and I want to clear this bad air between us and trust you to do what I hired you to do. It wouldn't make sense for me to hire you to be the troubleshooter, then not let you *troubleshoot* issues when they arise. So, I'm taking a step back."

"Well, that's a first," Royal said.

"Don't make me change my mind," Ramsey said.

Romulus glanced at Ramsey, then said, "Don't worry, Royal. He's not going to change his mind as long as he has Gianna to occupy his time."

"Even if I didn't, I still need to trust Royal to do his job. Now, let's get ready to meet with Dan."

"Alright," Royal said standing.

Romulus followed Royal out of the office.

Regal stayed put. When the office door swung closed, he asked Ramsey, "So, what's the latest? Did she agree to marry you?"

"I haven't heard anything yet. I instructed Felicity to tell her about my proposal today. She's probably telling her right now, as we speak."

"Do you think she'll go for it?"

"I hope so."

"You like her *that* much?"

Ramsey's eyes beamed with joy and truth. "Yes, I like her *that* much."

"Then I need to meet this girl."

"You'll meet her when I convince her to come to one of our family dinners."

Regal's eyes brightened. "You want her to meet mom and dad?"

Ramsey's smiled widened at his brother's shocked expression. "Yes, but only as my wife."

"Oh, then I'm going to that bakery tomorrow. I have to meet this woman, ASAP."

"That's cool. Maybe if you meet her, you'll

understand my obsession—I mean attraction—to her, but even if you don't understand, I don't care. She's my girl."

"Whoa," Regal said with his palms up in front of him. "Okay, Ram. I get it, but if it all goes as you plan, wouldn't you want your girl to get along with the family, especially mom? You know she'll have to pass the mom test."

"She will, but I'm sure mother would just be happy that I'm married. She wouldn't give any consideration to the details of how it happened as long as it did."

"True," Regal responded. "Whatever the case, I'm heading to the bakery tomorrow. It does open on Saturdays, right?"

"Yeah."

"What's the name of it again?"

"The Boardwalk Bakery, at the University City Boardwalk right across from Chico's."

Regal frowned. "Chico's? What's Chico's?"

"It's a women's clothing store, but since you've never heard of it, you probably won't know where it is. So, do you know where The Wine Cellar is or House of Leng? Any of those ring a bell?"

"Oh, yeah. I know where House of Leng is."

"It's the building next to it. You'll see Chico's. The bakery is right across from there."

Regal stood up. "Cool. I can't wait to see what little miss cupcake is made of."

A smile altered Ramsey's lips and a vibrant glow sparkled in his eyes when he replied, "She's made of everything in this world that's sweet."

Chapter 11

BUSINESS WAS GOOD at the bakery this Saturday morning as it usually was on Saturdays, but especially today since the weather was forecasted to be in the late seventies—early eighties. The bakery was fifty percent filled with customers and Felicity was there too, helping Gianna. She'd just taken another batch of cupcakes from the oven.

Business was great. Gianna, not so much.

Officially burnt out, Gianna sat in the office doing computer work while Felicity manned the front counter and took cupcake pans from the oven.

"Hey chica," Felicity said peeping around the door to Gianna's office.

Gianna looked up at her. She'd been massaging her tired eyes with balled fists.

"You look a mess, Gianna. Go home and let ya girl handle this."

"No, I'm fine. I just need to figure out some things here."

"Girl, go home. You've already baked enough cupcakes to feed all of Charlotte so it's not like I'm going to run out. Let me handle it. I know you're worried about Gemma anyway so..."

She was worried about Gemma. When was

she *not* worried about Gemma? Harriet didn't work on weekends, and it bothered Gianna to leave the house in the morning while Gemma was still sleeping. "I am worried, but I'll call her."

"I'm sure she's fine," Felicity said.

Gianna frowned. Already tense, she snapped, "How can you be sure she's fine? You don't know her like I know her, Felicity."

"I'm just trying to console you somehow. To be your friend. I don't want you freaking out back here for no good reason."

"Let me worry about me, okay? You...just...just leave me alone for a minute."

Felicity didn't say a word more. Gianna's stress level was already up, she knew, so she simply turned and walked away.

Gianna picked up her cell and dialed Gemma's number.

She didn't get an answer. She dialed again.

No answer.

She glanced at the clock. It was 10:35 a.m. That was early for Gemma so maybe she was still resting. Gianna closed her eyes. Took a breath. She couldn't panic now – not when she was on the verge of losing her business. Her house. And now she had to contemplate Ramsey's proposal. How he would magically make all of her problems go away if she agreed to marry him. She massaged her throbbing temples , angling her head down, catching sight of the $2,100 she owed Queen City Properties. While she could desperately use the help, she wouldn't allow money to be a motivating factor in determining if she would marry someone.

* * *

Regal stepped inside of The Boardwalk Bakery, taking in the pink walls – black tables and black and white tiled floors. The place wasn't crowded like the small ice cream shop just a few doors away but it had a good amount of people with kids stuffing cupcakes into their little mouths. But it was the woman behind the counter that caught his attention – that made his heart skip a beat. Wow!

"Jeez, she's beautiful," he said under his breath as he approached the counter. He smirked. He should've known Ramsey's girl would end up being breathtaking. Ramsey always preached about being attracted to someone's heart – their soul – yet this woman was an exquisite beauty who looked exotic with her full lips, big eyes and high cheekbones.

He licked his lips. *Dang. What am I doing? I can't be attracted to my brother's girl.* He smiled to himself and shook his head, still taking in the features that were slowly taking his breath away with each step he took towards her. Her hair was in a net, but it didn't hinder the lovely features of her face. Her eyes were a rich mocha brown. Skin – a thick, lickable chocolate.

Lickable. Really, Regal? Pull yourself together. This is Ramsey's girl, and he better be glad he saw her first.

Felicity's frown deepened as the man got closer to the counter. She knew the guy was in some way related to Ramsey. They looked too much alike *not* to be related. What she couldn't figure out was why he was staring at her like she was a juicy piece of watermelon. And did Ramsey really send a member of his family here to check up on her progress with Gianna? To see how she was coming along in getting Gianna to sign his proposal? The very thought incensed her. How dare he.

Fighting back irritation, she forced herself to say, "Welcome to The Boardwalk Bakery. What can I get for you?"

"Oh, I didn't actually come to get a cupcake. I—"

"I figured you didn't. You're here because of Ramsey, correct?"

Regal squinted. "That's correct. Ramsey is my brother. I'm Regal. I told him I was going to come down here today so I can meet you." He didn't know what to make of it just yet, but the chick seemed pissed about something. This couldn't be her normal demeanor, could it? Felicity's eyebrows shot up to the ceiling. "So you could meet me? Why do you want to meet *me*?"

"Well, for obvious reasons. My brother—"

"Okay, let me stop you right there, Randy."

"It's Regal."

She rolled her eyes. "Whatever. You can waltz right on up out of here and tell Ramsey I don't need him sending human drones down here to spy on me. If he wants to know how I'm doing, he can bring his butt down here himself."

Regal frowned. Confused. *This* was the woman his brother was infatuated with? A slick-at-the-mouth broad with an attitude problem? And she was still glaring at him with her mean, pretty self. Regal was all for respecting women and even though this woman had a bad attitude, he would still respectfully leave, but not without offering her a few words of his own. "I know Ramsey wanted a wife, but jeez—I didn't think he was desperate enough to settle for one with an attitude problem. I'm sorry I wasted my time coming down here."

It wasn't until he made the statement that Felicity realized the misunderstanding here – he was looking for Gianna, not her, and he must've thought she was Gianna since she was working the cash register.

"Excuse me," she said.

Regal was steps away from the door when he decided to turn back around as it seemed her voice was projecting toward him. "Yes? Do you have more venom to spew at me?"

She smirked. "It's not like you have the best attitude, so whatever. Anyway, I think you're looking for my friend Gianna. She's in the back. In her office."

A smile grew on his face and relief settled in his chest. "You're not Gianna?"

"No. I'm Felicity..."

"Felicity...the Wedded Bliss chick?"

Felicity narrowed her eyes. "How do you

know about my business?"

"Ramsey told me all about it. It's definitely not something I would ever try but me and Ramsey are two completely different people. Now, where is the office so I can meet my sister-in-law?"

"Don't you think you're being a little presumptuous? Gianna hasn't agreed to marry your brother yet."

"She will."

Felicity crossed her arms. "And how can you be so sure?"

"It's been over a decade since I've seen a spark in my brother's eyes when he talks about a woman. It's there every single time he mentions Gianna. Now, where is she?"

Felicity rolled her eyes, not thrilled with his persistence. "I'll go get her." She turned away and immediately felt his presence, the heat of his body right behind her. She turned around and nearly growled when she said, "Customers are not allowed back here."

"They are when they're related to the owner."

"Good grief you're just as annoying as your brother."

"I'll take that as a compliment coming from a smart-mouth chick like you."

"What's that supposed to mean?"

"Just what I said." Regal looked amused at the frown lines disturbing an otherwise beautiful face. And if she knew what was best for her, she'd take the pout out of those lips or he'd do it for her.

"Hey what's going on out here?" Gianna's said emerging from her office with her keys in one hand and purse in the other. She looked at Felicity first then her eyes landed on the tall man beside her who looked like a Ramsey knockoff – same complexion. Same height. "Are you...Regal?" Gianna asked.

"I am," he said. "How did you know? Did Ramsey give you a heads up that I was coming?"

"No. I just remember he said he's closer to you than he is with your other two brothers. Wha-what are you doing here, Regal?"

"I just wanted to meet you but your evil friend borderline jumped me in the lobby."

Gianna glanced at Felicity and attempted to hide a grin but it showed through, anyway.

"I'm going to go back to the front, Gianna, before I have to put *somebody* in their place," Felicity said, sizing Regal up.

"Come put me in my place, girl. I'm ready."

Felicity kept on walking, ignoring him.

Regal looked at Gianna and asked, "Is she for real?"

"Yes. It takes her a while to warm up to people, especially men."

"Oh well... I didn't come here for that. I came to meet you, Ms. Gianna."

"I'm glad you did, Regal and I wish I could stick around and talk to you but I have to go home and check on my sister."

"Gemma?"

Gianna looked surprised. "Ramsey told you about her?"

"Yes. In fact, there is no need for you to go check on her. Ramsey is out to breakfast with Gemma as we speak."

The color fell out of her face. "Say what?"

"My brother didn't call you this morning?"

"He did but I assumed he was calling...calling to ask me if I had an answer to...um..."

"His proposal?"

She connected her eyes to his gaze. "You know about that, too?"

"Sure do. How about we step inside of your office so we can talk for a minute?"

"Okay," Gianna replied. Returning to her office, she sat at the desk.

Regal sat in the chair next to the desk.

She looked up at Regal then a soft beautiful smile came to her face.

Regal watched her for a moment, acquainting himself with her delicate features. Like her friend, she too was beautiful but she appeared exhausted. "What are you smiling about, Gianna?"

"Nothing," she said. "Um...you look so much like him. It's like I'm looking at Ramsey, but not really."

Regal flashed a lopsided grin. "Yeah, me and Ram look the most alike out of the four of us."

"So, he kidnapped my sister this morning, huh?"

Regal chuckled. "I wouldn't call it kidnapping. His exact words to me were: *no, I'm not playing golf this morning. I'm taking my sister-in-law to breakfast.* And yes, he did say *sister-in-law*."

Gianna shook her head, blushing. "Are you a fairly reasonable man, Regal?"

"More reasonable than my brother if that's what you're asking."

She smiled. "Yes. That's what I'm asking. Don't you think what he's asking of me is absurd."

"No. Not for Ramsey."

"Why not?"

"Because that's the way my brother is. He's a risk-taker. You didn't know that? He's jumped out of more airplanes than a new recruit of navy seals. He parasails, white water rafts—the crazier the river, the better."

No, she hadn't known all of that, another reason why she shouldn't accept his proposal – she really didn't *know* him. "So, I'm a risk for Ramsey. Is that what the appeal is?"

"No. My brother genuinely likes you, Gianna. I just met you and I think you're perfect for my brother. I get good vibes from you, unlike your friend out there."

"Oh, don't pay Felicity no mind. She's a good friend to me. She comes here every Saturday to help me at the bakery after working her own job."

"Is that right?" Regal asked.

"Yeah. That's right."

"Well, that's nice of her, but let's get back to the reason why I came here. You and my brother."

"Yeah, your brother who kidnapped my sister," Gianna interjected to say.

Regal smiled again. "You are an adorable little thing aren't you?" he asked.

"Don't try to sweet-talk me. In fact—" She whipped out her cell. "I'm going to call Ramsey and give him a piece of my mind."

Regal chuckled. "He'd just gobble up your words just like he does with your cupcakes."

Her eyes narrowed.

"My brother is like a shock absorber when it comes to disagreements and disputes. And I know for a fact that the only reason he took Gemma to breakfast is because he didn't want you sitting here worried since Harriet doesn't work on Saturdays."

"Or maybe he's trying to convince my sister to go along with his plan."

"What plan?"

"To marry me. He's been planning this whole thing from the start. From the moment we met. What I can't figure out is why he chose me."

"I can assure you this wasn't planned. If it was, I would have known about it. Ramsey thinks something led him to you. To this bakery. It was a shock to him when he found out you and Felicity were best friends, but his initial interaction with you, his connection with you is authentic. My brother only misses our monthly, Sunday meals for urgent matters and I'm assuming he missed last Sunday because of you."

Gianna thought for a moment, remembering that Sunday was the day Ramsey rescued her from embarrassment at the grocery store. The day he was supposed to be buying ranch dressing for the Sunday dinner Regal was referring to. "Well, whatever the case, Regal, I never wanted to get married in the first place because I didn't think I was *marriable* in addition to a crapload of other reasons."

Regal smirked. "You said you weren't...marriable?"

She grinned. "Yes, and I know that's not a word. Look, the bottom line is, I don't know the first thing about having a boyfriend let alone a husband."

"Well, you better learn fast because Ramsey is not going to let up. Consider this your fair warning."

She felt her stomach cinch. "You know another thing that bothers me about what Ramsey told Felicity to relay to me?"

"What's that?"

"He told her to tell me all the things he would do for me *if* I accepted his proposal. Like, if I marry him he'd erase all of my debts. First of all, I don't like a man paying my way. Second of all, it feels like blackmail to me and I refuse to be blackmailed."

"Wait...he said he'd take care of your debts *after* you agreed to marry him?"

"Yes, his way of persuading me to sign."

Regal smiled. How could it be classified as blackmail when Ramsey had already started paying off things for her? She obviously wasn't aware of that. "It's not blackmail, Gianna. I know because, per his instruction, I cut a check to Queen City Properties a week ago."

Gianna frowned. Queen City Properties was the name of the property management company where she had leased this space for the bakery. "What does that have to do with me?" she asked Regal.

"The name Queen City Properties doesn't ring a bell to you?"

"It does. I have a lease with them for this unit. I was just sitting here racking my brain trying to figure out how I was going to pay the bill."

"Well, you don't have to rack your brain for at least the next ten years. My brother has prepaid the lease for that long."

Gianna snorted before she burst out in laughter. He couldn't be serious, could he?

"You can't call it blackmail after all, especially since Ramsey has already begun paying things off for you."

The smile fell from Gianna's face when she watched the serious expression on his. She logged into her account with Queen City Properties and noticed the balance was zero, when just earlier in the week, it was in the negative: -$2,100 to be exact. She glanced up at Regal then back to the screen. She saw a note added to the account that read:

This account has been prepaid for the next 10 years. Check received from Ramsey St. Claire (of St. Claire Architects) in the amount of $122,100 (includes past due amounts for June and July as well as the late fee).

Shock took over her features. A soft gasp left

her mouth.

"By the look on your face I take it now you understand how serious he is about you."

Stunned, all she could do was stare at Regal before hiding her face behind her hands, sobbing.

"No, no, no," Regal said standing up. He wrapped his arms around her and said, "There ain't going to be none of that."

"I just don't understand why he's doing this for me." She sniffled.

"I'ma be honest with you, Gianna. I don't understand *half* of what my brother does. I really don't, but it always seems to work out somehow."

Gianna sniffled again.

"I never thought I'd see the day when I saw him so taken by a woman again. By you sweetheart. I see this whole bizarre interaction between you two as an even swap. You need a little help here and there and he enjoys your company. The only thing you're missing is time. You don't know him as well as you want and he seeks to know you better. From the looks of things, you two are already off to a good start."

Gianna smeared tears down her cheeks. "We weren't off to a good start. I'm sure he's told you about our crazy date."

"He did. However, even that wasn't a deterrent for him. He likes you, woman," Regal said, palming her shoulder. "And now, I see why. You're sweet, unlike your friend out there. What is she like on sugar high or something?"

He chuckled. "I hope you keep inventory on those cupcakes because she's probably tearing them things up when you're not looking."

Gianna laughed, her tears drying up now.

"Are you okay, Gianna?"

"Yes. I'm okay."

"Good. Ramsey will have my head if he thinks I made you cry."

Gianna frowned as if she didn't believe him especially since she'd never seen an aggressive side to Ramsey.

Regal stood up. "I have to get going now, but it was an absolute pleasure to meet you, Gianna."

"You as well, Regal."

"I hope this won't be the last time we see each other," he said. "Oh what am I saying? Ramsey's got you. I'm sure I'll be seeing you again," Regal said standing in front of the office door where Gianna had joined him. From where he stood, he could see Felicity frosting cupcakes.

Felicity glared at him.

He smirked.

Felicity could hear him as clear as day when he asked Gianna, "Hey, Gianna, do you mind if I use the back exit so I don't have to walk by Miss Wedded Bliss?"

Gianna chuckled. *These two...*

"Miss Wedded Bliss?" Felicity said, eyes narrowed. She wasn't about to let that slide. "How about you leave the same way you came in? You're a man aren't you?"

"Yeah. More than you can handle."

"Oh, please," she said waving him off. "Take your ego somewhere else. We don't need your super-high level of testosterone around here."

"Maybe I'll bring it to Wedded Bliss so you can find me a wife."

Felicity laughed. "Don't waste your time. I can spot husband material just like that and you're definitely not it."

"And I suppose you're wifey material," he said. "I've already seen your neck snap, crackle and pop more than a bowl of Rice Krispies."

"Yeah, and what kind of grown man eats Rice Krispies?"

"What kind of grown woman slams down all of her best friends cupcakes?"

"What?"

"Huh?"

"Ugh..." Felicity had enough of the tit-for-tat. "Weren't you on your way out?"

"Okay, break it up," Gianna said, standing next to Regal as he towered over her.

"Sorry about that, Gianna."

"Where's *my* apology?" Felicity asked Regal.

Before he could respond, Gianna took one of the freshly frosted cupcakes and said, "Here, Regal. Have a red velvet cupcake."

"No thanks, sweetie. I don't eat cupcakes."

"Maybe you should start selling Rice Krispie treats, Gianna," Felicity said tickled.

Regal glanced at her then took the cupcake Gianna had offered to him. "Thank you, Gianna."

You're welcome."

"Wait a minute," Felicity said. "He didn't pay

for that."

She just couldn't leave it alone.

"It's okay," Gianna told her.

"No, it ain't. He gets no special privileges just because he's Ramsey the Great's brother."

"Felicity..." Gianna began.

"She's right," Regal said. He took out his wallet and removed a twenty. "Here you go," he told Felicity. "I see your hands are full right now. Should I tuck it inside of your bra?"

"Yeah, if you want to get slapped."

He chuckled. "A slap from those small, soft hands will feel like a massage to me WB."

Gianna grinned to herself. Regal had just met Felicity and already he knew how to push her buttons.

"My name is not *WB* or *Miss Wedded Bliss*. It's Felicity."

Amused, Regal handed the money to Gianna instead. "Throw the change in your tip jar. I thought I saw one out there."

"Yeah, there is. Thank you, Regal."

"You're welcome." He looked at Felicity and said, "I'll see you next week, WB."

"Whatever." Felicity continued frosting cupcakes.

Regal gave her frame a full once over before he finally exited.

Chapter 12

"So, WHAT IF your plan doesn't work?" Gemma asked, staring intently at Ramsey from across the table as they sat in The Pancake House. Ramsey had ordered her a large bowl of grits and a small orange juice while he ate a meat omelet with a side of hash browns.

Ramsey took a long sip of coffee, then he looked across the table at her. Studied her. She looked much happier today for some reason. Her expression didn't seem so drab. Even her eyes appeared brighter. She had a pink scarf tied around her head that matched the colors of the flowers on the summery blouse she wore. "Does your question imply that you're okay with the idea of me and Gianna being together?"

Gemma smiled. "I am. However, I'm not sure Gianna will be okay with it."

"Why are you okay with it, Gemma?"

"Because I think you're a good person. You're just what my sister needs to loosen up a bit." Gemma wiped her mouth. "That was delicious. I haven't had grits in forever." She took a sip of juice.

"Why am I what she needs?"

Lowering the glass to the table, she said,

"Because, I've taken up Gianna's whole life. She needs to get out there...experience life outside of Charlotte. Shoot, she needs to experience Charlotte. She never does anything. Well, besides work. And you look like you've done it all."

Ramsey pulled his phone from his shirt pocket to see the caller: *Cupcake*. A smile appeared on his face.

"It must be Gianna," Gemma said watching him.

He glanced up at her. "It is. I haven't talked to her since Felicity laid out my proposal yesterday, so this should be interesting." He cleared his throat and answered, "Hello, beautiful."

"Hi, Ramsey." She sniffled.

He frowned.

"Is something wrong?" Gemma asked when she saw the disturbed look on Ramsey's face.

Ramsey shook his head, but something *was* wrong. Gianna was sniffling. Had she been crying again? Returning his attention back to the phone, he asked, "How has your day been so far?"

"Okay." She sniffled again. "Your brother stopped by here and told me you kidnapped my sister."

Ramsey chuckled softly. "I didn't kidnap Gemma. She's sitting here having a good time with me. Would you like to speak with her?"

"Yes, please."

Handing Gemma the phone, Ramsey said, "Hey, she wants to talk to you."

Gemma took the phone from his grasp and said, "Hey, Gianna."

"Don't *hey me*, lil' girl."

"I'm not a *little girl*, Gianna. I'm nineteen, going on twenty."

Ramsey smiled.

"I tried to call you. You had me all worried that something had happened to you. You don't answer your phone, don't bother returning my call and I have to find out from Ramsey's brother that you're out to breakfast."

"Okay, I should've told you. I just forgot. It was a spur-of-the-moment thing. But don't worry. Your fiancé is taking good care of me."

Fiancé...

Ramsey gave Gemma the thumbs up for that statement.

"He's not my fiancé," Gianna said.

"Then, he should be. He really likes you."

"So, you two *have* been talking about me."

"Of course. What else are we going to talk about? The weather? Anyway, I'm going to get back to breakfast. I'm having a delightful time with Ramsey. You want to speak with him again?"

Gianna rolled her eyes. "Yes."

Gemma handed Ramsey the phone and said, "She wants to talk to you again and she's a lil' pissed."

Ramsey took the phone and said, "See. I told you everything was fine."

"You should've told me you were picking her up today, Ramsey."

"Check your phone. I tried to call you this

morning, but you didn't answer because you were assuming I was calling about the proposal that Felicity presented to you, correct?"

"Yeah, but—"

"But that's not why I was calling you, sweetness. I was calling to inform you that I was taking Gemma to breakfast. Even after I couldn't sleep last night because I thought you'd be so turned off by my proposal, I still somehow managed to get out of bed to pick up lil' sis because I knew Harriet was off today and you'd be at work worried about Gemma being home alone. I didn't want you to worry. All your worry, anxieties and anything else that keeps you up at night should be filtered through me going forward."

The line went disconcertingly quiet.

"Gianna?"

He frowned when she didn't answer him. Then he heard her sniffle. Heard her whimpers. He stood up and said, "Excuse me for a moment, Gemma. I'll be right back."

"Okay," Gemma replied.

Taking the call outside, he said, "Gianna, I didn't mean to upset you."

"I'm not upset, Ramsey," she said in distorted words.

His eyes were closed when he said, "Then why are you crying? You're breaking my heart."

"Because these things you do for me...I don't...I don't know why you're doing them and I feel like I don't deserve your kindness."

"I want you, Gianna. I want to get to know you. I want you, and your sister, to be a part of my family."

"Why?"

"Everyone deserves a family, don't you think, and you're a part of mine now whether you sign those papers or not. You always will be, so you may as well say yes."

She sniffled again.

"Just hearing you upset is doing something to me. I don't want to see you or hear you upset anymore. You deserve more, and now you have it. I don't want you to sign a prenuptial agreement or anything to that effect. What's mine is yours and I'm prepared to give you the world, Gianna."

She sniffled again.

"I'm not asking for an answer right at this moment. In fact, as hard as it is for me to do, I'm staying away from you this weekend so you can have some time to think about it. But I *will* see you on Monday, not because I need an answer, baby, but because I'll need to see you."

Gianna remained quiet, speechless, not knowing what to say to this man.

"Gianna?"

She sniffled. "Yes?" she replied softly.

"Did you hear me?"

"Yes."

"I'm going to go back inside with Gemma now. I'll talk to you later."

"Okay."

He pressed the red 'end-call' button on his phone and released a long, slow breath, then he walked back inside the restaurant.

Gemma smiled at him as he approached the

booth.

"Is everything okay with Gianna?"

"Yes. She's okay."

"What about you?"

He flashed a grin. "What about me, Gemma?"

"You have a weird, glazey look in your eyes."

"Glazey? You and your sister love making up your own words, huh?"

She giggled.

"Nah, but I'm okay. Your sister just gets to me...to my soul."

"Why?"

"You wouldn't understand it if I explained it to you."

"Can you try?"

He thought he owed her that much. "Do you remember when I told you I know what Gianna is going through in reference to your situation with the cancer and all?"

"Yes."

"I was in Gianna's place. I was the one taking care of my sick fiancée at the time. Her name was Leandra. She had lung cancer like you, and the surgery, I think, would've saved her life. But there wasn't enough money back then...I couldn't afford it," he said frowning. He'd always been angry with himself for that. Could never forgive himself for failing her. "I couldn't *afford* to save Leandra even though I loved her. I loved her deeply, Gemma. I just couldn't...I couldn't save her. We were young, in our mid-twenties. I was still in college. I didn't have a steady job. I was working part-time while going to college full-time. My parents had exhausted all their funds and resources to help pay for Leandra's chemotherapy. Her parents didn't have money like that, so it was all on my family to take care of her. Unfortunately, chemotherapy didn't work for her and she...she died. After eight, long, agonizing months, she died in my arms and I don't mean that in a figurative sense, Gemma. She literally died in my arms. I was holding her when she expelled her last breath."

Gemma felt a chill run through her. "Oh my God. That's so tragic."

"I'm not going to let you suffer the way she did and I'm definitely not going to allow Gianna to suffer the way *I* did. That's why I need you to be on board with your new plan of care because once it's started, we're going in full force to kick this cancer in the butt."

"I'm ready," Gemma said.

Ramsey smiled, then reached across the table to shake her hand. Her small hand clasped onto his and he slowly shook it.

"Ooh...I like your watch," she said, glancing at it.

"You want it?"

"No, silly," she laughed. "That's a Rolex. I could buy a car with that thing."

Ramsey looked at the watch that he'd paid $15,000 for. "Yes. You could. As a matter of fact, you need a car, so—" Ramsey undid the clasp on his watch and put it on her arm. The watch was loose, dangling around her tiny wrist. "When we get you better, you'll get a car."

She giggled. "Now, you're reaching. I have to get better, first."

"And you—we—have a good shot at this, Gemma. Do you see how much happier you are today than you were last night? In fact, this is the happiest I've seen you since we met."

"I know. I feel it, too."

"You know what's changed?" he asked her. "It's hope. Last night, I gave you hope. Today, you're much better. See how that works?"

"Yes. I see," she said, fiddling with the watch.

"You have big arms, Ramsey. This watch is waaay too large for my arm. Look, I can even get it over my elbow."

Ramsey chuckled.

"And I don't want to trade it for a car. It means something to me. It means...hope."

"Then, by all means, keep it, sweetie. You'll get a car either way."

Gemma stood up and walked to his side of the table and while he was still sitting, she wrapped her fragile arms around his neck and said, "Thanks for being the big brother I never had."

"Thanks for being the little sister I never had."

Chapter 13

GIANNA ALMOST BROKE her neck getting inside of the house to talk to Gemma. She was so in a hurry, she tripped over the top step and bumped her head on the storm door. "Ouch!" she said, rubbing the area where she was sure a bruise would form.

Gemma opened the door. "What in the world? Sounded like somebody was trying to break into the house."

"That was my head hitting the storm door. I was trying to get in here so fast, I tripped."

"Why? Curious to hear about my breakfast with your boyfriend, huh, or shall I say your fi-an-cé?"

"Whatever, Gem. One thing is for doggone sure...I'm not making any hasty decisions when it comes to this proposal. I'm sure he took you to breakfast to convince you to convince *me*, huh?"

"No. He actually just wanted to tell me about it and ask for my opinion. So, I gave him *my* opinion."

Gianna took a long look at her sister. Something about her was different, in a good way. She appeared more lively and upbeat. "How are you feeling, Gem?"

"I feel good."

Her forehead creased. "You do?"

"Yes. I do. It's like, ever since Ramsey told me about treatments that can cure me, I for once feel like I can beat this thing." Gemma sat on the sofa and brought her knees up to her chest.

"Ramsey told you about what treatments?" Gianna asked, joining her sister on the sofa.

"Surgery, among other things."

"Things we can't afford."

"We can now. He already said he'd pay for it. He said he'd do anything for you and by proxy, that means me as well."

Of course he'd said that. He told her the same thing.

"And you agreed to this?" Gianna asked.

"Yep. Sure did. We shook on it and then I hugged his thick, good-smelling neck."

Gianna's mouth fell open. "All this time I've been trying to get you to try, Gem, and you talk to me like you were ready to give up. Then, all of a sudden, Ramsey comes along and you're ready to be all in."

"You know why, Gianna?"

"No, explain. Please."

Fiddling with the platinum, diamond encased watch on her dainty wrist, Gemma said, "You were struggling. I was the cause of those struggles, and I knew you couldn't afford to take care of me and the bills and everything else. So yes, that's why I was giving up. But Ramsey gave me hope. That's what this watch represents. Hope."

"He gave you his watch?"

"Yep."

"Let me see that."

Gemma handed the watch to her sister.

Gianna looked at it and said, "This is a Rolex."

"It *is* a Rolex, Captain Obvious. What gave it away? The letters R-O-L-E-X?"

Gianna giggled. Gemma was getting her sense of humor back, it seemed. Coming down off laughter, Gianna explained, "I'm just wondering why he gave you such an expensive watch."

"I'm sure he has others, now give me my hope back."

Gianna laughed when Gemma snatched the watch from her grasp.

After sliding it back on her arm, Gemma said, "He wants to take me to the cancer treatment center in Atlanta. He says he'll make the appointment and everything. Of course, I wanted to discuss it with you, first."

"I would love for you to go there, Gem. Trust me when I say if I could afford it, you'd be there already."

"Now, you can afford it."

"No, *Ramsey* can afford it."

"And thus, you. He already looks at you like you two are an item. I don't know what kind of spell you put on him, but he thinks the world of you, Gianna."

"I honestly didn't do anything to warrant any attention from him. I'm usually a nervous wreck whenever he's around me. Today, I met

171

his brother, Regal, and found out that Ramsey paid the lease on the bakery for the next ten years."

"Oh shoot...you know what that means."

Gianna blushed. "It means he paid the lease for ten years."

"Which, in turn, means that whatever he's starting with you, he's looking for it to be long-term."

"And that's why I have to put a stop to this. I can't have him doing all this stuff for me on a whim because he feels some special connection to me. Connections get short-circuited and a man like Ramsey St. Claire who can have any woman he wants gets bored easily." Gianna stood up. Stretched. "Anyway, I'm going to talk to him later to let him know I need more time to think this stuff through and I can't do that with him hovering over me, being my bill fairy and kidnapping my baby sister for brunch."

"Kidnapping...ugh...you love to over-exaggerate, don't you? And don't call me a baby. Just say I'm your younger sister. *Little* sister is even acceptable."

"I like baby sister better." Gianna stood up and kissed Gemma on the cheek. "I'm going to take a shower. I'll be back down to make you some soup."

"I already did it."

"You did?"

"Yep."

"Then I guess I'll be back to make myself some dinner."

"And I'll be in my room. If I fall asleep, don't

be all up in there kissing my cheek either."

Gianna laughed. "I'll kiss your cheek all I want, lil' girl," she said, then headed upstairs.

Chapter 14

SHE WANTED TO call Ramsey before she took a shower, but she decided to take a shower first, hoping to settle her nerves in preparation for his sexy, over-the-phone, smooth-as-silk voice. She didn't want to be *talked into* doing anything and he was the kind of guy who could talk a woman into doing anything he wanted her to. That's why she had to get a handle on her nerves. Put on her game face. Or game *voice*. Whatever...

She had to prepare for Ramsey like she was studying for a quiz. Her plan – to tell him she couldn't marry him. That wasn't much of a plan but that's all she had. While she supported Felicity's dreams of opening her own matchmaking company, the whole Wedded Bliss concept of getting married to someone and getting to know them *after* the fact was a bit of a reach for her mind to grasp. But then again, so was Ramsey. Garnering the attention of a man like him was a long shot, and he'd come to her, not vice versa. He strolled into her bakery and had let it be known that he found her interesting. That he liked her. That *like* somehow morphed, grew legs and turned into a marriage proposal.

Before she lost the last few nerves she had left, she dialed his number, listening as it rung, waiting to hear him answer with his usual, *hey, Cupcake* greeting. The phone rang again and her heart raced. She pushed out an even breath then said softly, "Why am I stressing? Chill out, Gianna. He's just a man. Don't let him get you all flustered. He's not actually here. He's just—"

"On the line, sweetness," Ramsey said.

"Oh my God!" she shrieked.

He chuckled. "What were you doing, Gianna? Preparing yourself to talk to me?"

"Ugh..." she turned red in the face. Shouldn't she be used to him by now? And why the heck was she flushed? He wasn't actually there.

"Gi-a-nnaaaaa?" he sang.

She panicked, hung up the phone and hid her face behind her hands. "What's wrong with me?"

The sound of her phone buzzing unnerved her even more. She knew it was him calling back. "Okay. You can do this," she told herself. She picked up the phone telling herself to ease into the elephant-of-a-conversation they needed to have but when she answered the phone, tact and ease flew out the window as she spewed out, "I can't marry you."

"Tell me why."

"Because I can't."

"You can. Tell me why you don't want to."

"Well, for...for obvious reasons."

"I don't want to hear the *for obvious reasons* copout when the reasons to me aren't so obvious. I want you to tell me why?"

She frowned. "Okay. We hardly know each other."

"I feel like I've known you all my life."

"But you haven't. Not even for a month yet, and I don't want to feel like you're coming to my rescue like you're a Wonder Pet or something."

"A what?"

"Never mind," she said, realizing he didn't get her cartoon reference.

"And I'm not coming to your rescue. I'm helping you."

"Same difference."

"No, it's not, Gianna. You're helping yourself. You're running a bakery."

"Yeah, a bakery I wouldn't have if you hadn't swooped in and paid off the lease."

"You're welcome, by the way."

"Ramsey—"

"You're welcome, by the way," he repeated.

Ugh. "Thank you," she finally said.

"Anything for you, Gianna. And I mean, anything."

Gianna sighed. How was she going to get him to reason when he was being so freakin' nice in a take-charge kind of way? She had to try because she knew she couldn't marry him. Taking another approach, she said, "Okay...give me one week to—"

"No," he said before she could get the full request out.

"You don't even know what I was going to say."

"I heard *give me one week*, and I didn't need

to hear the rest."

"Ramsey, please let me finish."

She could hear him release a sigh.

Absorbing his frustration, he said even-toned, "Okay. I apologize. Please, continue."

"Thank you. Now, what I was saying was, I need a week to think about this—one full week without seeing you or talking to you. That way, you can be sure that this marriage thing is what you really want and I can make a good decision without feeling rushed. That's all I'm asking."

"Are you finished?" he asked curtly not wanting to interrupt her again if she wasn't.

"Yes. That was it."

"The answer is no," he responded.

"Ramsey—"

"I *will not* go a full week without seeing you. Are you kidding me? I haven't seen you Friday, Saturday and I hadn't planned on seeing you tomorrow because I wanted to give you time to think. But a week...no. Not going to happen."

"You're being unreasonable."

"Maybe I am."

She sighed heavily.

"What's so bad about being married to me, Gianna? Huh? Am I not your type?"

"I don't have a type. I've never had a type."

"Then tell me what the problem is."

"I told you what the problem was. You just refuse to listen to me." She held her head out of frustration. "I'll talk to you later. I have to go."

"Why all of a sudden?"

"Because you're not listening to me, Ramsey."

"Don't hang up on me again. I *am* listening to you. Just because I don't accept what you're saying doesn't mean I'm not listening. I want you, Gianna."

"And you always get what you want, right?"

"Yes. That would be correct."

She thought quietly.

Trying to think of reasons he assumed was causing her so much anxiety – things she was probably too embarrassed to mention, he said, "I won't touch you. Kiss you. I won't initiate anything unless it's your wish."

Yeah...that's what you say now.

"Gianna?"

"Yeah?" she said, sounding defeated.

He didn't like the tone of her voice. Not at all. "Alright, let's put that topic on hold for a minute. How's Gemma?"

"She's okay. She had a good time with you today. And you didn't have to give her your watch."

"I know. She liked it, so..."

"So, you just gave it to her."

"Yeah. I did. And, FYI, I made her an appointment at the cancer treatment center a week from today for an initial consultation with a doctor and he will determine whether or not she can have the surgery."

"You said a week from today?"

"Yes. Actually, the appointment is on a Wednesday. If she's eligible, she'll have the surgery a week after that and then stay at the center until every trace of cancer is gone. First, though, we need to get past the initial consultation."

"If she does have the surgery, how long could she end up staying at the center?"

"Probably about a month and a half. Maybe two."

That hit Gianna hard. It would take Gemma two months to recover?

"It's something to start preparing yourself for, and I'll be there with you every step of the way, Gianna."

"What about your work?"

"I can work remotely."

"You'd do that?"

He smirked. "You still don't get it, do you? I told you, I'd do anything for you."

"Yeah...anything except give me a week to think about your marriage proposal."

"I'm sorry, sweetness. Anything that involves taking you away from me doesn't fall into that scope."

Gianna went quiet again.

"What did you eat for dinner this evening?" he inquired.

"I haven't eaten yet."

"Then what are you going to eat?"

"Um...probably a can of sardines and some crackers."

"What?"

"Sardines. You know those little fish thingies in the flat can-looking thing—?"

"I know exactly what you're talking about. I just don't understand why *my* woman is eating prison food?"

Gianna snorted a laugh. "It's not prison

food. Prisoners probably wished they had a can of sardines. They're good, and since Gemma has already eaten, I'm just going to have it as a little snack for myself."

"Oh, Gianna, baby, you're destroying me."

She giggled. "It's fine, Ramsey."

"Please let me order takeout for you."

"No."

"Why not?"

"Because you're doing the whole rescue thing unnecessarily. Besides, I don't want takeout. I'm fine with what I got."

You may be fine with it for now, but no wife of mine eats sardines out of a can. And there was no doubt about it. She *was* his. Even if she didn't sign a thing, she'd still be his.

"Well, I'm going to let you get to your dinner. I'll struggle to get through the day tomorrow without seeing you, but I will see you on Monday for sure."

"Okay, Ramsey."

"You'll have an answer for me by then, won't you?"

"Don't know."

"You will. Sweet dreams, Gianna."

"Goodnight, Ramsey."

Chapter 15

RAMSEY RECLINED IN his favorite lounge chair on the deck. He told Carson that he didn't want breakfast. That was three hours ago. And now he was still on the deck outstretched. Sleep. Dreaming. In his dreams, he could see her face clearly – Gianna's face. He traced the delicate lines of her lips and licked his lips anticipating kissing her. He'd wanted to from the first – wanted to do things with buttercream she wouldn't dare dream of.

"Ramsey."

His eyes slowly opened, landing on Carson.

"Yes, Carson."

"It's noon, Sir. Can I interest you in a turkey and cheese panini with pimento?"

Ramsey stretched. Yawned. "What time is it?"

"Noon, Sir," Carson said for the second time.

"Yes. Lunch sounds good, Carson."

"Very well, Sir. Also, your brother said he'd be by in about ten minutes."

Ramsey didn't have to ask which brother. He knew it was Regal. "Okay. Thanks."

When Carson walked away Ramsey stretched his long legs before checking his phone. He saw the missed call from Regal.

"Don't remember the last time I saw you out here enjoying the scenery," Regal said, stepping out onto the deck.

"It's nice out here today," Ramsey said. "I actually took a nap. I haven't had a nap since 1997."

"Yeah, that's because you've been buried under a pile of work."

"Exactly. It feels good to have some downtime. In fact, it feels so good, I was thinking about extending it another month."

"Do it," Regal urged, sitting at one of the three patio tables. "It's not like you don't deserve it, man."

Carson brought out a tray of food and drinks. After the men both thanked him, Ramsey continued, "Truthfully speaking, the time off isn't for me."

"Oh. It's for her. Gianna."

Ramsey smiled. "So, you met her yesterday, right?"

"Ah, man...she's a doll. Voice sounded so sweet, she could lull a lion to sleep. Now, her friend on the other hand—"

"Felicity..."

"Yeah...that feisty little thing almost had me walking out of there."

"How's that?" Ramsey asked after taking a bite of his sandwich.

"Okay peep this...I walk into the bakery and see this woman behind the counter. I'm thinking she's Gianna but then the attitude came out of nowhere, man."

Ramsey chuckled. "That's Felicity, alright..."

"I know now. I thought she was *your* girl so you can imagine my confusion when she was nothing like you described. Then she realized that I thought she was Gianna and informed me that she was not. So, finally, I walk to the back to see my soon-to-be sister-in-law and she looked up at me with those golden brown eyes and said in the sweetest voice, *you must be Regal.* She's a breath of fresh air, Ram. She's perfect for you—to balance you out."

Ramsey nodded in agreement.

"I see what you mean about her being nervous, though. She was a little shaky and her eyes were red."

Ramsey's brows raised along with his protective antennas. "Red?"

"Like stress red. She said she was stressing out about some bills, and when I told her you paid the lease on the bakery, she started crying."

"She was crying? Ramsey said, dropping the sandwich back on the plate. "You made my baby cry?"

"No. *You* made your baby cry tears of happiness. I consoled her."

"Consoled her, her how?"

"Seriously Ram? I wasn't pushing up on Gianna. I just simply put my arms around her. I know she's yours."

Ramsey picked up his glass.

Regal narrowed his eyes to playful squints when he said, "You better be glad you saw her first, though."

Ramsey's gaze shot hollow point bullets at

his brother.

"I'm kidding, Ram. Jeez," Regal said grinning. "You look like you can kill me right now."

"I'm going to pretend the last two minutes didn't just happen," Ramsey said.

"Ram, you know I was kidding right?"

"Yeah, whatever. Anything else of note happening down at the bakery?"

"Not really. The place was fairly busy. Gianna looked tired. I mean, I don't know how she normally looks, but she looked exhausted to me."

That was how she normally looked and Ramsey wanted to do everything in his power to change that.

"Oh, and I told Felicity I was coming to Wedded Bliss so she could find me a wife."

Ramsey chuckled. "Get out of here, man. You told me I was crazy for doing it and yet you're going to give it a go?"

"Yep, just to annoy Felicity. I got something for that smart mouth of hers."

Ramsey shook his head. "Trust me when I say that's going to get old real quick."

"Nah. I like a challenge."

"Then you definitely have one."

"You're one to talk. You like a challenge, too...trying to get a woman to marry you so soon."

"Yeah...turned out to be more challenging than I thought."

"Why? Because you're used to women hanging on to your every word giving you what you want without any resistance?"

"Well, yeah."

The men laughed, then Ramsey continued, "But seriously, I may have to be firmer with her than I want to be, but I don't know how else to get her to want me as badly as I want her."

"And you're not talking about sex when you say *want*?"

"No. I mean, her—the woman."

"You could try to be a friend first."

"I consider myself a friend now, but I don't want to get stuck playing catch-up in the friend zone. Eventually, I'll need to know what her lips taste like—what parts of her feel like—"

"TMI," Regal shouted. "Too much information, bruh. You can stop that right there."

Ramsey laughed. "She's so scared of me and I want her to feel comfortable around me."

"Then invite her and Gianna over here to spend a week with you or something. Show her how you live, not in a flashy way but in a way where she'll come to understand your likes and dislikes. Your tastes. Who you really are as a person."

"Sounds like a good idea to me but she'd never go for it."

"She would if you weren't so cut-and-dry with it. You like the girl so reason with her. You're a business owner. She's a business owner, and she may be shy and all that but she's intelligent. Talk the language of business—since you're both like-minded in that way. Something tells me Gianna's not the type of woman to do things just because you throw money her way to pay this bill and that bill."

"She's not."

"Okay then. You know what you have to do, Ram."

Ramsey nodded. He knew what he had to do. The quandary was whether she'd go for it.

Chapter 16

"GIRL, IT AIN'T nothing like a good, black romance movie with some fine brothers that a chick can sink her teeth into," Felicity said. She was relaxing on the sofa at Gianna's house and they'd just finished watching, *Think Like a Man*.

"You mean that you can *dream* about sinking your teeth into." Gianna chuckled.

"Hey, either way it goes, my teeth got sunk."

Gianna shook her head, still smiling. "Okay...three sexiest black men in Hollywood. Go."

"Oh, that's easy," Felicity said. "Number one is my boo, Denzel Washington, of course."

Gianna laughed. "Why are women so infatuated with Denzel?"

"It's the eyes, girl. Those eyes and something about the way he licks those lips."

Gianna took a sip of the Irish Cream Felicity had brought over.

"Okay, who else?" Gianna asked.

"Girl, Michael Ealy, because when was the last time you saw a black man, in real life, with blue eyes? And that hard jawline...girrrl that's one fine specimen right there."

"Okay. One more."

"The dude who plays the president on *Scandal*."

Gianna snapped her head back. "Tony Goldwyn?"

"I don't know...the one Olivia calls Fitz or something."

Gianna laughed so hard, water came to her eyes. "I said *black* men, Felicity. Not white men who like black women on TV shows."

"Well, I'm just saying...the man is fine. He can come *Fitz* me."

"Okay, no more Irish Cream for you," Gianna said reaching for Felicity's glass.

Felicity moved her hand before Gianna could grab her glass. "I barely even touched this stuff. I'm not even tipsy. You know I'm naturally crazy."

"Yes. I know that all too well."

Gianna set her glass on the table, folded a leg underneath herself and sighed. "Welp, it's back to work for me tomorrow."

"Me, too, girl."

"I'm dreading it," Gianna admitted.

"Why?"

"Because I know Ramsey's going to show up. And it's not actual dread I feel. It's more like excitement mixed with a bit of terror and a fear of the unknown."

"Dang, girl. You should've just stuck with *dread*. And did you really just say, terror?"

"Okay...I'm not terrified of him, or men in general. I'm just super nervous. I've never even kissed a man, Felicity."

"Then we better start practicing."

"We?"

"I don't mean practice on me, silly." Felicity stood up. "I'll be right back."

She ran to the kitchen and was back within seconds with two red apples."

"Oh, no," Gianna said. "This can't be good."

Felicity flopped back down on the couch and handed Gianna an apple. "Okay, now hold the apple in front of you and picture Ramsey's face."

Gianna held the apple up and laughed. "I can't do it," she said, tickled.

"Yes you can. When Ramsey leans in towards you with those Denzel lips, you'll need to know what to do with 'em."

"I *do* know what to do? Run."

Felicity chuckled. "No, you ain't running nowhere. He's gon' make sure you can't run, especially when he has his arms locked around you. What are you going to do then?"

"I'll just have to ninja my way out of the situation."

Felicity laughed. "No. You need to pucker up, girlfriend. Now, hold your apple out in front of you, stick your tongue out and just lick it like this." Felicity demonstrated by using the sharpest point of her tongue to draw little circles on the apple.

"So, I'm supposed to lick his lips?"

"The tongue is involved in the kissing process, Gianna, whether you like it or not. You can't walk up to your man and press your lips against his and think that's enough. He's not a baby. He's a man. An alpha man at that. He'll need more aggression. You need to go all in. Has he tried to kiss you before?"

"We almost kissed at the bakery once, and he does stare at my lips a lot. Does that mean he wants to kiss me?"

"Yes! Now, stick your tongue out and let me see you work this apple."

"Ugh...I don't even know if I rinsed these off yet."

"Well, it's too late now. Stop stalling and get to licking."

Gianna pulled in a deep breath and forced herself to lick the apple like she was licking a popsicle. "Okay. I did it. What else?"

"Now, gently press your lips against it like this." Felicity demonstrated.

Gianna, once again, followed her instructions. "Wait aren't my eyes supposed to be closed?"

"You can close them if you want."

Gianna closed her eyes, pressing her lips all over the apple. Before she knew it, she bit a good size plug out of the apple and started chewing.

"You bit his lips off!" Felicity said, laughing hysterically.

"You laugh, but this is what I do with apples," Gianna said, taking another bite.

"Okay, but when Ramsey comes at you with those lips, don't say I didn't try to help you."

"I'm not worried about it. He won't kiss me. He knows I can't handle it."

"If you believe that, you're more naïve than I thought."

"He won't. I can't even be within a few feet of him without my hands twitching."

"And that's a turn on for men like Ramsey St. Claire." Felicity placed the apple on the table and picked up the glass of Irish Cream. "If you think Ramsey ain't going to kiss you, you must be out of your mind. Let me just keep it all the way one hundred with you, Gianna. He's obsessed with you."

Gianna laughed. "He's not."

"He is. When he talked to me that day, telling me to lay out his terms about this marriage proposal, he had *the* most determined look in his eyes. It freaked me out for a minute."

"So, tell me what you think about him, Felicity, and be honest."

"I will," Felicity said. "I don't like him that much. There. I said it."

"Why don't you like him?"

"Because he comes across as arrogant and I *do not* like arrogant men."

"So, you would prefer a pushover."

"No, that's not what I'm saying at all. Just because a man isn't arrogant doesn't make him a pushover. But that's beside the point. It doesn't matter whether or not I like Ramsey. It's all about you, honey bun. Do you like him?"

"I do."

"Then why are you frowning?"

"Because, I—I don't have much experience with men and he's very, um..." Gianna sighed. Unable to think of a word to describe him, she continued, "I talked to him on the phone last night. Although I know I'm going to say no, I told him I needed a week to think about the proposal—a week so I can get myself together enough to say *no* to him. I know how pathetic that sounds, but that was my plan."

"Okay. Continue."

"When I suggested the idea of taking a week to think this through, he automatically said, no. He's the kind of man who doesn't take no for an answer."

Felicity nodded.

"He's very...um...forthright. Precise."

"Aggressive," Felicity added.

"Yes. Aggressive. He sets his sights on something and he gets it. His sights are set on me for the moment, but I have a feeling that it's only a temporary thing."

"If that's the case, why would he want to marry you, especially without a prenuptial agreement or anything. He just wants you."

Gianna thought about it for a moment. She didn't know what to make of it.

"Look, the bottom line is, Ramsey came to Wedded Bliss looking for a wife. He's found you and he wants to marry you."

Gianna leaned over, clenched herself, holding her stomach.

"Oh, get over it already," Felicity said.

"How can you tell me to *get over it* when you just admitted that you didn't like him?"

"I didn't say I didn't like him. I said I didn't like him *that* much."

"In your honest, professional opinion—do you think he's a good fit for me?" Gianna asked.

"Nope."

"Felicity!"

"I don't, not with your quiet, mild ways and his outgoing, risk-taking, arrogant ways. But, like I said, he seems to really like you so maybe he won't be that way with you. I don't know. It's hard to tell."

"And I'm supposed to be able to tell *after* I marry him?"

"Yeah. See, the reason the Wedded Bliss concept came to me in the first place was because—"

"Of your parent's divorce."

"Right, and because of the things my mother said to me right after. I was seventeen...I didn't understand why they were splitting up. I just remember her going on and on about how much he had changed. She said he wasn't the same man he was before they got married."

"We've had this conversation before, Felicity, and I'll say the same thing I've been saying over and over again. People change. You can't tell me that you marry someone with the expectation that they would never grow and change."

"You're right, and it also adds to my vision of establishing this business in the first place. People—men and women—like to make good first impressions when they go out with someone, especially for the first few times. Then, as weeks turn into months, they start to get comfortable. Like, for instance, the woman may not care if every single strand of her hair is perfectly in place before she sees her man, and the man doesn't mind looking a little rough and unkempt because the first impression phase is over. Wedded Bliss bypasses all that first impression crap. You meet someone, you like them, you get married. Then there's no more, *oh, he's not the man he used to before we got married*. Or *marriage changed him*. It's just two people growing together and not falling apart."

"Yes, but it's mainly based on how a person looks, Felicity. People go through profiles and probably pick the best-looking person they can find and all of a sudden they have a soulmate?"

"Well, for some people, it's based on looks," Felicity said. "For others, it's based on their actual profiles. Their likes. Dislikes. Hobbies."

"And for Ramsey?"

"For him, it was based on a woman having goals. Or in his words, a *thing* she loved to do. He wanted a woman who wasn't *fake*, he said. He told me he sees hearts, not faces and as crazy as it sounds, I do believe him. The major thing I don't like in this whole ordeal is when I asked him how I was supposed to get you to sign the papers. His comment was for me to relay to you everything he was willing to do for you—like pay off your mortgage, your car, the lease on the bakery and get Gemma the best medical care possible – but only *after* the papers were signed. That pissed me off."

"Would it make you feel better to know that he's already paid the lease on the bakery for the next ten years as well as the past due amount?

He took Gemma out to breakfast Saturday morning since Harriet was off and he knew I would be at the bakery. Said he didn't want me to worry. And, he's already been in contact with a cancer treatment center in Atlanta to schedule an appointment for Gemma. She's so excited, Felicity."

"Wait...he's done those things already?"

"Yes, and as you know, I haven't signed a thing."

"Wow," Felicity said, at a loss for words. "Wow. I'm—I'm shocked."

"Why?"

"I just—I didn't—"

"You didn't think he would do something like that for me?"

"No, not until you signed the papers. Guess I figured him all wrong."

"Um, newsflash, Felicity—ever since you broke up with Demontae, you've been extra hard on men."

"I have not."

Gianna smiled. "Oh, yes you have. You just threatened to slap Ramsey's brother yesterday, the very same day you met him, mind you."

"That's because he was bothering me." Felicity finished her drink and set the glass on the table. "What kind of name is Regal, anyway? His parents named him after a freakin' Buick. I wonder if that's where he was conceived."

"Ew, okay, moving right along..."

"If he has a sister named Lexus, I'ma know something." Felicity laughed.

"There is no sister. All boys. Four, total."

Felicity quirked up her lips. "Whatever. I know one thing...if he calls me *Wedded Bliss* again, I'ma call him *Buick Regal*."

"You wouldn't," Gianna said, tickled.

"Watch me."

After catching her breath, Gianna said, "I'm not coming to Regal's defense, but at least the first letters of his name don't spell out *demon* like Demontae."

"Dang," Felicity said like that had just occurred to her.

"Besides, I think Regal likes you."

"Why do you think something insane like that?"

"When he walked away, he looked you up and down."

"A lot of men look ya girl up and down 'cause they trying to determine why I'm not all girly and flirty even though I look like I should be."

"Now, that's funny. *You're* not girly? Every time I see you, you're wearing a different shade of MAC lipstick, and when you come to the bakery to help me, you're wearing pumps. I done told you not to come up in there wearing heels, but no, you'd rather risk spraining an ankle than wear a pair of comfortable, safe sneakers."

"That's just a matter of preference. It has nothing to do with being girly. Listen here...you just need to make sure you have some smear-proof lipstick on when Ramsey comes at you with those lips."

Gianna's stomach fluttered. "Stop it, Felicity."

"And now that I know Ramsey's not the complete and total jerk I thought he was, I say he's absolutely perfect for you."

Gianna nodded, thinking about how Ramsey had already gone above and beyond for her. How when he'd first come into her bakery, he didn't go running for the hills, even after she was admittedly acting crazy. He'd stayed, ordered a cupcake. Gave her a generous tip. The next day came another tip. He'd paid for her groceries, followed her home and helped her unload and unpack them. He rescued her from being drenched when she showed up at the bakery as the sky opened up with a downpour of rain. He brought items to help her bakery run more efficiently. He helped sweep. Mop. He took out an ad to attract more customers to her bakery. He hired a nurse. Covered copays. Took Gemma out to breakfast and gave her hope in the form of a Rolex, but hope nonetheless. He was making an effort to be there for her. What had she done to be there for him? What did the man who had it all need?

"My God," she said evenly having reached an epiphany.

"What is it?" Felicity asked, watching her friend's eyes grow bigger.

"He really *does* want me."

"Duh," Felicity said. She laughed. "Look, you have a decision to make and since Ramsey ain't giving you no time to think about it, I'ma mosey on up out of here and go home. You can bet your next batch of cupcakes that he's gon' roll up there to the bakery tomorrow."

"He is. He's already warned me." Gianna said standing.

Felicity reached to hug her and said, "May the force be with you, child."

Gianna giggled. "Text me when you get home, silly."

"Yeah. Text me during those heart palpitations you're going to be having tomorrow when your man shows up."

"If that's your way of asking me to tell you how it goes, I'll call you tomorrow."

"Alright. Later."

Gianna watched Felicity walk to her car and on a whim, she ran there as Felicity took a seat.

"What did I forget?" Felicity asked.

"Nothing. I was wondering if you had the paperwork with you."

"What paperwork? The Ramsey stuff?"

"Yes."

"Yeah. It's in my briefcase. Why?"

"Give 'em to me."

"You're signing?"

"Yes. Give 'em to me, and hurry up before I lose the nerve. Gimmie, gimmie, gimmie."

"Oh...wow. Okay," Felicity said, opening her briefcase, taking the forms out. "I can't believe this is happening."

Gianna took the forms from Felicity's grasp and signed them – all five of them. "Is that it?"

"That's it." Felicity couldn't wipe the grin from her face when she said, "You know after Ramsey signs and I submit these, you're officially going to be Mrs. Gianna St. Claire."

Knots formed in her stomach. "Yes. I realize that. I'm sure at some point I'm going to faint."

Felicity could only laugh. "You're not going to faint. You're going to fall in love. That's what you need, anyway. Some love and affection."

Gianna smiled at the thought of being loved. It was a good feeling. She could only imagine how it would be when it actually happened. When she felt loved, adored and cared for. When she belonged to someone. To Ramsey.

Chapter 17

MAYBE IT WAS her unsettled nerves at the realization that Ramsey genuinely wanted to marry her or just the fact that she'd been working nonstop and needed a break. Whichever the case, she didn't feel like working at all today. She wanted to go home, curl up in her bed and sleep. Unmotivated, she didn't even bother making a specialty cupcake today. She only made the daily's – vanilla, chocolate, butter pecan and lemon.

Her first customer had arrived right after opening. A few more strolled in afterward. She was still getting used to this much traffic in the morning. Those ads Ramsey placed must've been paying off.

When the bakery's phone rang, she took the cordless from the pocket of her apron and answered, "The Boardwalk Bakery. How can I help you?"

"Hi, is this Gianna?"

"Yes. May I ask who's calling?"

"This is Judy from St. Claire Architects. How are you?"

"I'm good. How can I help, Judy?"

"My boss wanted me to order eight dozen butter pecan cupcakes for an upcoming meeting this week."

Gianna smiled. She didn't have to ask Judy who her boss was. "What day is the meeting?"

"Wednesday."

Good. That will give me plenty of time to make ninety-six cupcakes.

"Is that doable?" Judy asked.

"Yes. It is. What time do you want to pick them up?"

"Oh, you don't deliver?"

"No. I'm a one-woman operation over here."

"Oh, that's fine. I can come pick them up," Judy said. "I'm not far from there."

You're not? "Where are you located?"

"IBM Drive, right off of Harris Boulevard."

"Oh. Right," Gianna said. How did she not know that? IBM Drive was a hop, skip and a jump (okay, maybe two jumps) from J M Keynes Drive where her bakery was located. Ramsey's office was located *that* close to her bakery?

"Hello?"

"Oh, sorry. Thank you for your order, Judy. I'll have it ready for you."

"Wonderful. I can't wait to try one. My boss brags about them...says they're the best he's ever had and he doesn't even like sweets."

Gianna blushed. "In that case, I'll be sure to make them extra special for you guys."

"Aw. Thank you."

"No problem. Have a good day, Judy."

"You do the same."

Gianna wrote the order down and stared down at her note. She knew she wouldn't have gotten this order if it wasn't for Ramsey. She looked up when the doorbell tinkled and saw Jerry walk in.

"Hey, Jerry. I was just talking about you the other day. Where have you been?"

"Oh, I've been around. Here and there. You know how it goes."

She walked around the counter, hugged him and said, "Let me go get you some cupcakes."

"No, sweet thang. That's okay. I didn't come here for cupcakes."

Gianna's forehead creased. "No?"

"No. I just stopped by to see how you were doing?"

"I'm doing okay."

"I see you got some customers in here dis moanin'."

"Yeah. Things are picking up."

"I see. Looks like you done changed some thangs up 'round here, too."

"Yeah. I had some help with that."

"Hmm..." Jerry said. "Well, it's nice. How's little sister?"

"She's okay. Still struggling through, but yesterday, I actually saw her smile, so that's always good."

"That's good. Very good. If she's anything like you, I know she has a good spirit on her."

"Thank you, Jerry. Now, let me get you some cupcakes."

"I done told you I didn't come here for that."

"Oh, hush. I got plenty of lemon cupcakes made. I'll be right back."

"Alright."

Gianna hurried to the back, prepared a half dozen cupcakes in a container and walked back to the front. "Here—"

Her words halted at the sight of Ramsey sitting at *his* table. *Their* table? No, *his* table, just sitting there. How had he slid in so covertly? She couldn't have been gone for a minute. It was almost like he'd known the exact moment she stepped away. Had he been watching her from outside? From his car perhaps?

"Are you alright, sweet thang?"

"Ye-yeah. I'm okay," she said. At least she didn't drop the box this time. A small improvement. "Here you go, Jerry."

"Thank you."

"You're welcome. Enjoy the rest of your day, okay."

"I will. You do the same, sugar."

Jerry offered a single wave to Ramsey then they talked for a brief moment before Jerry exited.

Gianna swallowed hard. Her heartbeats sped up something awful at the very sight of Ramsey sitting there. Was he *really* sitting there, or was she just imagining it? Gosh, he had her thrown off balance. She glanced around the bakery, looking at her other customers and then back over to where Ramsey was sitting.

Crap, crap, crappity crap! He's here. Like actually here. Breathe, Gianna. Breathe. Caught in the magnificence of his hypnotizing presence, all she could do was look at him. He hadn't shaven in the few days they hadn't seen each other, and the hair on his face, sweet Jesus, it made him look so much more manlier as if he needed to be any more manly. He was as manly as men came – a sophisticated beast-of-a-gentleman with a heart for the shy cupcake girl. And he was sitting there looking utterly sexy in a black, short-sleeved, button-down shirt that gripped the muscles of his thick arms and a pair of tan chinos that had the grown-man fit to them. He didn't have on socks, just a pair of black-grained Gucci loafers with gold detail.

With his chin resting on his large, interlocked hands he looked at her. No, he wasn't looking. He was gawking. Analyzing. Seeing who was going to make the first move. Who was going to smile first? Say *hi* first? Who was going to break the ice? Why was there ice that needed to be broken? It's not like this was their first time speaking. They'd been through too much in the last three weeks to be starting over. To be playing ping pong with their eyes. But every encounter with him felt like a new beginning. Was that normal? Or was this feeling something that only the two of them shared?

He's waiting for me to initiate. I know he is. Think, Gianna. Think. Then it dawned on her. Just give the man some coffee and a cupcake. He'd like that, right?

"Right," she said softly. She walked to the back and retrieved one of the freshly frosted lemon cupcakes then took a large cup, filled it with coffee and added three creams and three packs of Splenda to it. After securing the lid on the coffee cup she walked toward his table. His gaze seemed to sharpen as she approached, so instead of maintaining eye contact, she used his watch as a focal point until she lowered the coffee and cupcake to the table.

"Thank you, Gianna," he said, looking up at her.

"You're welcome, Ramsey," she said, barely looking at him.

"Can you sit with me for a few minutes?"

Instead of answering him verbally, she pulled out a chair and sat down. She glanced up at him. Why wasn't he talking? He was still staring with that serious expression on his face – no doubt the same look he gives to his counterparts when he's on the verge of closing a deal or making a decision that required full mental awareness. She knew he wanted to bring up their conversation from last night and his proposal and everything that came with it. It was on the tip of his tongue. But just when she thought he was going to begin his negotiations, he asked, "What happened here?" and touched the small bruise above her right eyebrow.

"I—I walked into the storm door when I got off work Saturday evening. It doesn't hurt...just looks bad. I'm fine."

In the mildest tone he could muster, he said, "I've missed you."

She looked up, held his vision. Surprised – surprised that he missed her after only three days and surprised that the first thing out of his mouth wasn't proposal-related.

"I've missed you too, Ramsey."

Surprise lit up his features as well. He was surprised she missed him, too, after three days and even more surprised that she admitted it. "You did?"

"Yes. You look as if you find that hard to believe."

"I do. You're always nervous and jumpy around me. I get the feeling that when I'm not around, your breathing pattern returns to normal, your eyes are not dilated and you're not in panic mode."

She smiled. "You would be correct, but that doesn't mean that I don't like having you around." She held his gaze, surprised herself at how long she was able to do so – a new record – then decided to address the matter at hand by saying, "I don't know how I'm supposed to marry you when I'm not comfortable around you, Ramsey. I'm not, and I'm just being honest." Yet, she'd signed the papers – but he didn't know that.

Ramsey took a sip of coffee. This isn't what he wanted to hear. He wanted to hear a resounding, resolute *yes* from her. Instead, he was getting something that sounded like *it's not you, it's me*. "Then we need work together to find a resolution, Gianna, because I can't walk away from this—from you. I can't."

"I don't want you to, Ramsey," she said softly.

"Then what do we do about it?" he asked, lowering his coffee cup to the table and reaching to hold her left hand, caressing it. "What do I need to do to make you more comfortable with me? To make you trust me?"

She shrugged. "I guess I would need to spend more time with you."

"Okay. You work full-time, even on Saturdays. How do we spend more time together, sweetness?" he asked before bringing her hand up to his mouth, kissing the back of her hand, watching her close her eyes as he did so.

And something amazing happened. Instead of freaking out, having a spasm of nerves contort her body, she opened her eyes and kept them on him, even as what felt like a wave of energy passed from his body to hers. In his eyes, she saw a deep, dark pit of desire. Of need. Of true longing.

"How do we spend more time together?" he asked, still holding her hand.

"I don't know, Ramsey."

"I've been thinking about this all night and the only solution I could come up with is for me to move in with you, or for you and Gemma to come and stay with me, and before you completely shut me down, I would sleep on your couch if I were to stay with you...whatever's necessary. And, if you were to stay with me, I'd give you and Gemma your own private guest bedrooms."

Gianna smiled. "You're serious, aren't you?"

"I am."

"You know if I agreed to stay with you, I'd have to drive from Lake Norman every morning to open the bakery."

"I know, which is why I'm offering to stay with you, instead."

Gianna thought about it for a moment before her mind went on to something else. "A woman named Judy, from St. Claire Architects, called me this morning."

"Judy's my secretary. Why are you changing the subject?"

"Because Judy told me something that made me realize how one-sided this relation-friendship between us has been. She told me that St. Claire Architects, your business, was located on IBM Drive. I didn't know that, and I think I should've known that just like you know where I work. Where I live. I should've known that your business was two miles down the street from mine."

"What are you saying, Gianna?"

"I'm saying you've been so good to me and trying your best to learn things about me and I haven't been making that same effort, so I want to start. I want to know who you are. I think you're a wonderful man, Ramsey, and I truly appreciate everything you've done for me and Gemma, and it's time that I do something for you. So, yes, I will stay with you for a week."

A smile came to Ramsey's face. "Is this effective today? Please say yes."

She smiled beautifully. "Yes."

He released her hand and something that sounded like a moan of satisfaction came out of his mouth. "Did you really just say yes?"

Her smile blossomed. "I did."

He moaned again, looking heavenward as if his prayers had been answered.

"I have to get back to work," she said as two customers walked in. "Are you going to stick around for a while?"

"Do you want me to stick around for a while?" he asked her. Still holding her hand, he could feel it twitch just slightly when she replied, "Yes."

"Then, I'll stick around for a while, sweetness."

She tried to pull her hand from his grasp but he tightened his grip on it and held eye contact with her. "Are you going to release me, Ramsey?"

"I don't want to." He brought her hand to his nose and pulled in a long inhale of her sweet scent.

"Don't lick my finger," she teased. "There are customers in here."

"So, if there weren't any customers, are you saying I could?" he asked, then chewed on his bottom lip.

Gianna watched his lips move. "Yes. I mean, no. I have to get to work. I'll talk to you momentarily."

"See that you do." He watched her walk away. She had on a pair of blue jeans today and black shoes with a purple T-shirt. And, as always, her outfit was hidden behind a black apron. He watched her interact with her customers. She would glance over at him from time-to-time as he drank coffee and finished off the lemon cupcake. The taste of her frosting today did something sensual to him, probably because while he was wide awake last night trying to think of ways to reach her without being too bold and forthcoming, he imagined using his index finger to paint frosting on her lips and kiss it off. He would do it one day. When the opportunity presented itself. When he knew she could handle it.

He glanced up at her. Smiled.

She smiled back, then returned her attention to the door. A few customers exited and one entered.

Ramsey finished up the first cup of coffee then broke his gaze away from Gianna to look at his cell phone. It was the cancer center. He answered quickly.

"Ramsey St. Claire. How can I help you?"

"Yes, hi, Sir. I'm a patient advocate calling about your upcoming appointment for a Gemma Jacobsen."

"Is there a problem?"

"Well, I'm calling to inform you that we do not accept private insurance."

Ramsey rolled his eyes. He never mentioned anything to anyone about insurance when he'd called before. "That's fine."

"Okay, so you're prepared to pay for the visit out of pocket?"

"Yes. I'm prepared."

"Because if you need to reschedule, you'll need to let me know today."

He was getting more irritated by the second. Then he glanced up at Gianna and watched her wave at a little girl – a little girl with two pigtails wearing a dark blue, white and yellow sundress. The girl was adorable, but it was the look in Gianna's eyes that caught his attention. He could see someone as sweet as her with a child—his child. There was no doubt in his mind that she would be a good mother and he'd give her all the babies she wanted.

"Sir?"

"I'll pay in full when we get there," Ramsey told the patient advocate who sounded more like a *hospital* advocate. A make-sure-they-got-their-money-in-advance advocate. "Was there anything else?"

"No. We look forward to seeing you next Wednesday at 9:00 a.m."

"Perfect. Thank you."

"Thank you. Have a good day."

Ramsey placed the phone on the table then looked up when he saw Gianna approaching.

"I brought you some more coffee," she said.

"Thank you, sweetness, but you don't have to serve me. I came into your life to serve you, not vice versa."

"Well, it's the least I can do for the man who is trying to save my sister's life." Still standing next to him, she felt a sudden urge to reach out and touch his face and the prickly hair that had grown in there, but she was too timid to do so. "Would you like another cupcake?"

He smiled naughtily. "I have a taste for something sweet, but not another cupcake."

"Then, what would you like?" she asked.

Her naïveté had his heart thudding. She was completely unaware that he was coming on to her. "How about a go at your lips?"

"My...my lips?"

"Yes."

"Um...uh...I gotta go check on the pies. The cakes. I mean cupcakes," Gianna said nearly breaking out into a sprint to get away from him. A kiss? No way. She'd turned into mush if she pressed her lips against his. And she was certain that once he got those lips on her, he wouldn't want to let go. A small peck on the lips wouldn't be sufficient like Felicity had warned her. He'd want the whole shebang. Her entire mouth. A sensation ran through her at the thought that he could desire her that much. If she had hair on her arms, it would've been standing straight up.

Ramsey simply smiled as he watched her run, thinking how nice it would be to corner her so she couldn't run. The cupcake girl had passion inside of her that had never been released, and he was certain that he could open those floodgates. It was only a matter of time.

Chapter 18

AFTER GIANNA HAD packed up enough clothes and personal items that she and Gemma would need for a week, Ramsey requested that Gemma ride with him to which she happily obliged. All the while they were conversing about her upcoming appointment now that she was confirmed for next Wednesday, and he kept looking through the rearview mirror, making sure Gianna was staying close.

The feeling of knowing the woman he intended to marry would be staying at his home – that would ultimately become *their* home and in his mind already was– was producing a feeling of elation deep within his soul. Her being here felt right. There was no question about whether or not she was the woman he wanted. She was it.

Walking inside, they were greeted by Carson with ice cold, sweet tea served in crystal glasses. Ramsey had already given Carson the heads up that he would be having two women over for the week. He could only imagine what the man must've thought – probably that he was going to be a participant in some strange threesome – but it was nothing of the sort. He had finally gotten his sweetheart on his turf and if all went well, she'd never leave. The one-week offer was never intended to be just for one week. He wanted Gianna for an eternity – her, her baggage, her problems, her heart, her soul and anything else she had to offer. Everything.

"Um...Ramsey, I would love to tour your massive mansion, but I'm pooped," Gemma said. "Can you show me where I'll be sleeping?"

"Sure thing, Gem," Ramsey said.

"Allow me, Sir," Carson stepped in to say, then winked at Ramsey.

"Thanks, Carson," Ramsey told him.

"Wait, let me get my hug first," Gianna said walking over to Gemma and gave her the most tender, compassionate hug. "I love you, sweet girl," she said softly.

"Love you, too." When they parted, Gemma said, "Goodnight, Ramsey."

"Goodnight, Gemma."

"Oh, and don't keep her up too late, Ramsey," Gemma said. "You know she's a lil' cuckoo in the mornings."

Gianna smiled at her sister. She couldn't deny the truth, so she just went with it.

"I'll keep that in mind," Ramsey said. He looked at Gianna, extended his hand to her. "Shall we continue with the tour of the house?"

"Uh...okay," she said, reaching for his hand, feeling heat stir in her abdomen.

They headed to the kitchen first – a gourmet kitchen. A chef's dream kitchen. The granite island was big enough to be an actual island –

the thing was huge – about the size of a king-sized bed. And the quality craftsmanship of the woodwork in the kitchen was impeccable. That detail alone must have cost a small fortune. The wood floor was so shiny, she could see her reflection in it. And then the soft ceiling lights gave the kitchen a welcoming, homey feel.

He showed her the expansive living room areas – one of which looked like a showroom that no one used – decorated with high-end furniture. The other was more of a family room but still had an expensive feel to it with its wall-mounted flat screen, fireplace, furniture that looked so comfortable, it drew you in and the view – oh goodness, the view. He said he had converted the sunroom to a family room. This was amazing. And equally as amazing was his home gym. It was a step away from the family room and had that same view of beautiful Lake Norman.

The next room he showed her was his private office. It too had its own lake view and a large table that contained several blueprints and sketches, she noticed. And on one wall, there was an expansive bookshelf with all kinds of books on architecture and design. Situated on the opposite wall was a wet bar and a leather sofa, two matching chairs and a coffee table.

He watched her as she looked around, pleased with the awe on her face. He liked the fact that she was impressed. He liked it even more that when she got off work, she'd changed into one of her summer dresses – a plain cotton, dark pink one that hugged her body and accentuated that small waist he couldn't wait to grip. "What do you think?" he asked to hear what she'd been showing in actions translated to words.

"You have a beautiful home, Ramsey."

No, we have a beautiful home…

He took her up to the second level to show her the four guest bedrooms, one of which belonged to Carson. He showed her where she would be sleeping for the week, right next to Gemma's room. All bedrooms came with their own private bathroom.

"So which bedroom is yours?" she inquired.

"I was wondering when you were going to ask me that," he said. Still holding her hand, he took her to another set of stairs, hidden behind a door with a keypad lock. He punched in a code and they walked up the stairs together, hand-in-hand and once at the top, he stepped into his bedroom – a grand master suite that encompassed the entire third floor.

"Wow," she said, taking it all in. The room was filled with elegant décor with a black and cream color scheme. The four-poster bed was fit for royalty and looked like the perfect escape after a long day. The wall facing the lake was made up of windows and there was even a set of French doors that led out to a balcony.

"There's a balcony?"

"Yes. Do you want to see it?"

"Yeah," she said with a twinkle in her eyes.

Ramsey opened the door and she stepped out behind him, blown away by the sheer

216

beauty of the view. "Wow," she said a second time. "This is...this is breathtaking."

Ramsey came to stand beside her. As she took in the view, he admired her. She was the *view* that had his mind blown. And another thing that had him secretly filled with joy was, she had yet to grasp that this was all hers.

"Do you come out here a lot?"

"No. I'm usually on the deck downstairs. I only come out here to meditate."

He looked at her and wanted so badly to wrap his arm around her and claim her as his, then and there, but, again, he paced himself. He got her here at his house. He couldn't devour her just yet no matter how much he wanted to. "I can't tell you how happy I am that we'll finally have some time to get to know each other."

"Yeah," she said, but with less enthusiasm than he had.

When his cell phone rang, he glanced at it and saw *Wedded Bliss* on the display then told Gianna, "Take your time enjoying the view. I'm going to step inside to take this call."

And she was so enraptured by the view, she didn't hear a word he'd said.

Ramsey eased the French doors opened then stepped inside of his bedroom. "This is Ramsey," he answered.

"Hi, Mr. St. Claire."

"Hi, Ms. James...not getting your receptionist to do your dirty work today I see."

"Don't start with me today."

He chuckled. He could see her eyes rolling

already.

"Anyway, I was calling with some good news, or shall I say to congratulate you as I'm sure Gianna has already told you."

Told me what? And what news could be better than Gianna standing on the balcony of his bedroom? Agreeing to spend a week with him? He doubted that she could top that. "What news? What are you talking about?"

"Gianna signed the papers. When can I expect your signatures?"

Frowning, Ramsey looked through the glass to see Gianna looking up to the sky with her eyes closed. The breeze fanned her hair. *She signed the papers?* "She signed the papers?"

"Yes."

"When?" he asked, his breathing heavy.

"Last night."

Last night? After she told him she needed time? A *week* to think about it? And now she'd done a complete three-sixty and not only agreed to move in with him for a week, but to also sign the papers? "Are you trying to pull a fast one on me?"

"No. I'd play with you like that, but not my bestie. She signed it, and trust me when I say she's been hesitant to do so since I presented it to her on Friday, but yesterday, I believe she reached an epiphany."

"And what might that be?" he asked.

"That you really like her. She said it out loud with a look of astonishment on her face."

"She just realized that last night?"

"Yep, with a little help from me," Felicity

said. "When you made it clear to me that your intentions were pure, I knew she'd be in good hands. I could hear the conviction in your voice."

Still holding the phone, mind clouded in disbelief, Ramsey watched Gianna extend her arms and spin around in a circle. She'd actually signed the papers. "I'll be there in the morning to sign."

"What time?"

"What time do you open?"

"Nine."

"Then, I'll be there at 8:55 a.m."

"Okay. See you tomorrow."

Ramsey slid his phone back into his pocket and returned to the balcony. The moment he did, Gianna stopped twirling and her eyes opened. The closer he got to her, the wider they became.

"Ramsey?" she said when he didn't say anything. What was he doing? Why was he walking up to her with a hardened jaw and dark, pleasure-seeking eyes? "Ramsey, what are you—?"

Before she could utter another word Ramsey locked his arms around her and tried to steady her still enough to capture her lips but to no avail. She squirmed and flopped around like a fish fresh out of the water.

"Ramsey, what are you doing?"

"I'm trying to kiss you and I wish you'd hold still and let me."

"No," she said, gripping his dense wrists. "I can't kiss you."

Amused, he said, "Why not?"

"Because I was practicing on an apple and I bit it," she said amused and still trying to free herself from his grasp but feeling her legs grow weak when he tightened his hold on her and nearly lifted her off of her feet when he walked her backwards until her butt was pressed against the outer railing of the balcony.

He licked his lips and was staring at her lips when he asked, "You were learning how to kiss using an apple?"

"Yes."

Ramsey laughed.

"Stop laughing at me, Ramsey. It was Felicity's idea."

"Should've known. You're too innocent and smart to do something that silly." Ramsey licked his lips again. "Kiss me."

She frowned. "No."

"Wait...why are you frowning?" he asked.

"Because I don't want to kiss you," she said looking up at him with eyes that said the exact opposite of what she'd verbalized. She'd never been kissed before but had always been curious about how it would feel to literally merge her mouth with someone else's. Never in a million years would she have imagined that *the* mouth would be the likes of this man.

She chewed on her bottom lip, uneasy about it. She could even feel her lips trembling just barely and wondered if Ramsey noticed. He probably had with his extreme attention to detail.

Ramsey smiled, watching her intently as she

chewed on her lip. He knew what that meant, especially in combination with the things she wouldn't say that he could read in her eyes. Those light golden brown eyes with hints of green. Her eyes weren't dark. She wasn't mad. Afraid. She was curious and nervous, but mad? No way. "Why not, Gianna?"

"Because I've made a fool out of myself plenty times around you, Ramsey. You know how to kiss. I have no doubt about that. I don't. I know nothing. I don't know half the things you know about intimacy and kissing, touching and all of that stuff."

"Then let me teach you."

Her cheeks flushed. "No. I'm going to bite you. I know I am."

"Then bite me, baby. I'm game."

Gianna's eyes roamed him from up close. From every angle he was handsome. Gosh, he was handsome, and though she was nervous about it, she loved the way his body felt pressed up against hers. She gasped when his large hands settled at her waist.

"Gianna."

"Ye-yes, Ramsey."

"I'm the happiest I've been in a long time, and that's because of you. I enjoy your company, I'm elated that *you* made the choice to spend the week with me and right now," he said a breath away from her lips, "I'm *going* to kiss you."

"Oh no, this is happening," she squirmed in panicky breaths. "Make it stop, Gianna. Make it stop."

A soft smile came to Ramsey's face. "You're thinking out loud again."

"I—I am?"

"You are," he said looking at her with adoration in his eyes. "On second thought, let's postpone this. You're not ready, so—"

Before he could utter his next words, Gianna rose up on her tiptoes and pressed her trembling lips to his. The contact made sensations flood through her – sensations she'd never felt before. This was actually happening. Her lips were pressed to his. She could feel the prickly hairs of his mustache and with her hands, she touched his beard, loving the feeling of his wool-like hair beneath her hands. But was this how it was supposed to go down? Their lips just touching, not moving? Not doing anything but being pressed together? It felt awkward, and she knew that was her fault.

With their lips still mashed together, she opened her eyes and met his dark, stormy gaze. The sight of it jolted her back, and she gasped as she lowered herself to a normal stance.

"That's a good start, sweetheart," he said, "But I was thinking something more along the lines of this." He lowered his mouth to hers desperately seeking the taste of her tongue – anxious to see if she was as sweet as he imagined she would be. As he'd dreamed about time and time again. When he found it, that warm, buttery soft tongue of hers, he massaged it with his thick, heat-seeking one before sucking her tongue into his mouth, consuming her moans right along with it. He felt an intense pounding behind his ribcage as he tasted her this way, as he explored the recesses of her mouth. And oh how sweet it was.

It seemed time had stood still.

Gianna had never experienced a kiss before, but she had no doubt in her mind that this was the way a woman was supposed to experience a kiss – and not just the first one, but the subsequent ones to follow. A tingling sensation traveled through her and pooled at the juncture of her thighs. She moaned when she felt it. Was this normal to feel something—like down there—when a man kissed you?

Several times, she felt her stomach flutter, especially when his hands slid down her waist and cupped the soft flesh of her backside, squeezing her there. He was groaning loudly – almost needfully – and deepening the kiss so much, she could feel his tongue thrust closer and closer to her throat. She felt her breasts come alive, sizzling with awakening. Before they were just things she put in size 34-B bras. Now, they were blooming and tender, longing for his touch.

Now, that he'd lit a fire to her entire body, Ramsey deepened the kiss even further, steering her head to a slant to offer deeper tongue penetration, still lapping his tongue everywhere he could, making sure no corner of her mouth went untouched. He couldn't have that. He wanted it all. He even went so far as to graze his tongue across her teeth, into the hidden corners of her jaw and the roof of her mouth. And then, he was back to his favorite –

savoring her tongue – feeling it inside of his mouth. For him, this was the closest thing to perfection – so close he didn't know how he would let go of it. Of her.

And so he didn't let go. He tangled his tongue with hers and swallowed her moans – her sweetness – down his throat, wishing he could relieve the strain behind his zipper and take her right along with it. He hadn't expected the kiss – their first – to last this long or be this euphoric – so grandly exhilarating, he was getting high off of it. He didn't want to scare her off, but at the same time, he realized she needed to know what she was getting herself into. He was a passionate man and along with that came the responsibility for his woman to have that same level of hunger. Judging by the way she was moaning, he was certain he was on the right path to unlocking that desire.

Letting her tongue free, he sucked on her lips, giving them attention now, pulling them inside of his mouth with the slightest tug, sampling. He could never get used to this – her juicy lips, and sensuous tongue. The way her petite body felt against his. The way her shapely backside fit perfectly into the palms of his hands. Did she not know how much she turned him on from the first? How he longed to do this since sucking chocolate off of her finger. And finally, he got the chance to take lips, tongue, mouth – all of it like he'd never known what it felt like to kiss a woman.

Slowly ending the kiss, he left a few soft pecks around her mouth. At the last one,

Gianna opened her eyes, holding his gaze. She wondered what he was thinking.

He wondered what *she* was thinking. Was it too much for a first kiss? Why was there a mist in her soft, golden eyes? Before he could mentally ask another question, she wrapped her arms around his thick, muscular torso and squeezed, pressing her head to his chest.

He closed his eyes and circled his arms around her. What could be sweeter than this?

"We should probably go eat dinner now," he said, still holding her. *If we don't, I might just have you for dinner.*

"Okay, but first, may I have my tongue back, please?" she joked.

He laughed, then stared down at her after they'd parted noticing the smile on her face. "If by *your* tongue you mean *mine*, you can have it any time, any place and anywhere."

She didn't doubt a word he'd said.

He took her hand into his. "Now, let's go have some dinner."

"Okay. Can you give me a minute?"

"Why?"

She cleared her throat and said, "Nothing. I just need a minute."

"Why?" he asked again.

"I um...I have to wait for the feeling to come back to my legs."

He chuckled. "Are you serious?"

"Yes, I'm serious. You've kissed me weak."

His smile widened. *If you think that made you weak, then I can't wait to see what you do when I do other things to you.*

"And now, you have a satisfactory smile on your face," she observed.

"Why wouldn't I?" He leaned down, picked her up like a sack and threw her across his shoulder. "Now, let's go eat."

"Ramsey," she giggled. "Put me down."

"I will when we get to the dinner table." *I may just put you on top of the table.*

She giggled down two flights of stairs.

When he finally lowered her to her feet in the dining room, he pulled out a chair and said, "For you, my lady."

"Thank you," she said, feeling like she was floating. Being carried down two flights of stairs by the man who just kissed the breath out of her had her on cloud nine. She looked at the spread on the table. "Wow. Are you having company over? This is a lot of food."

"It is, but it's healthy food – therefore you need a lot of it. Well, *I* need a lot of it."

"And Carson prepared all of this?"

"Yes. He's a man of many talents. He takes care of most of the day-to-day operations around here while I handle business."

"I see."

Ramsey picked up a basket of wheat rolls and gestured for her to take one.

"Thanks," she said.

"You're welcome."

Gianna looked at the place setting and asked, "Is it bad that I can't tell the salad fork from the regular fork?"

"No. I didn't know any of that until I hired Carson. He likes to make sure I eat this way so when I'm entertaining clients, they won't think I'm not on their level."

"Oh. Okay. I don't feel so bad, then."

"Would you like some salad?" he asked her, holding the bowl.

"Yes, please." She watched him intently as he served her. He seemed to enjoy it. After serving her the salad, he added a serving of chicken cordon bleu to her plate, topping it off with a creamy mushroom gravy sauce.

"This looks really good."

"It does."

She pushed away from the table and said, "Before I start eating, I'm going to go check on Gemma. I'll be right back."

"Okay."

Gianna headed to the set of stairs right off of the foyer then walked down the long hallway until she found the guest bedroom where Gemma would be sleeping. She opened the door and saw Gemma sitting on a ginormous bed with pillows behind her back with her legs crossed, pointing the remote control to the wall-mounted, fifty-inch flat screen.

She grinned. "I thought you were sleeping, Gem?"

"Why would you think that?"

"Because you said you were tired as soon as we got here."

"I'm not tired. I just said that so you and Ramsey could have some alone time."

"Gemma!" Gianna said, still smiling. "How could you be so...so sneaky?"

Gemma chuckled softly. "I'm not going to be

a third wheel. Ramsey told me about his proposal."

"He did?"

"Yes."

"When?"

"On Saturday when he took me out to breakfast. He's totally in *like* with you."

Gianna smiled. If Gemma would've seen that kiss, she would've definitely changed like to love. Just thinking about it had her heart skipping beats.

"Go on. Go back out there and woo your man."

"Oh, please. I don't know how to *woo* anyone."

"Well, you did something right unless Ramsey just likes a lil' bit of *cray cray*, which he probably does."

Gianna chuckled. "What am I going to do with you, Gem?"

"Hey, just calling it like I see it. Now scat. Get out of here."

"You're okay? You don't need anything?"

"Nope. If I need anything, I'll call for Carson," Gemma said. "He told me he could be here lickety-split, whatever the heck that means. And he's already brought me a tray of food underneath that silver dome on the nightstand."

"Alright, well, I'm eating dinner with Ramsey in the dining room if you need me."

"And will you be spending the night in the king's quarters as well?"

"No, I will not!"

"Hey, it's a valid question."

"Alright, I'm outta here."

Gemma laughed. "Oh, that's all I had to say to get you to leave this room? I should've said that like five minutes ago, then."

"Bye, Gem. I'ma check on you before I go to bed."

"Okay."

When Gianna closed the door, Gemma took the plain white T-shirt she'd been using to disguise her coughs and coughed into it. It had become increasingly difficult to hide the coughing from Gianna and Ramsey for the past few days. And it had been the most difficult thing in the world to behave like she was suddenly feeling better when really, she'd felt herself getting worse. Felt worse for trying to keep up the act of being better. It drained her energy – what little she had – and now, she was coughing up blood.

She wiped her mouth then hid the shirt beneath the pillows. She picked up the Rolex – the hope – Ramsey had given her. She didn't lie to Ramsey. It did represent hope. Hope that Gianna would have the strength to move on after she was gone. Hope that she wouldn't suffer too much. Hope that Ramsey would forever take care of her big sister. Hope that her sister – who'd given up so much for her – would finally have someone returning the favor. Would finally have peace, contentment and happiness in her life.

* * *

"Is everything alright?" Ramsey asked the moment he heard her footsteps in the dining room.

"Yes," Gianna said.

Ramsey stood up and got her chair again.

"Thank you, Ramsey."

"You're welcome."

"Hey, you haven't eaten a thing," Gianna observed.

"I was waiting for you. I didn't want to be halfway done with my meal when you haven't even started on yours yet."

"Right. Okay." She picked up a fork. Then she lowered it and took the shorter fork in her hand.

"It doesn't matter, sweetness. Just use one."

"Okay." Using the short fork, she started on the salad first, glancing up at him. He'd started on his, too.

He ate more and was intentionally quiet. Testing her. She was opening up to him more, she'd signed the papers and she allowed him to kiss her senseless. Now, he wanted to see if she'd strike up a conversation with him in this setting.

"Ramsey, tell me more about your mother."

A smile settled in the corner of his mouth. "I told you a little about her already. What do you remember?"

"That her name is Bernadette. You said she was a chemistry teacher."

He appreciated that she was actually paying attention to him when he told her about his parents. "Yes, and she's been going on and on for the last fifteen or so years about how she has no grandchildren from her boys."

"I bet she would be a good grandmother—the kind who pumps the kids full of sugar and buys them noisy toys that need batteries."

Ramsey chuckled. "Yes. I can see that. Speaking of children, you never told me whether or not you want any. I think that's an important conversation to have with my *wife*."

She smiled. "Felicity told you I signed the papers, huh?"

"Yes. Why didn't you tell me?"

She shrugged.

"Don't shrug it off. Tell me."

She looked up at him, frowned slightly then stared back down at her dinner plate.

"Gianna?"

"Yeah?" She looked up at him.

"Tell me."

"I didn't tell you because I wanted to give you time to change your mind."

"I told you I wasn't going to do that."

"You don't know that," she told him. "You can't predict the future. Tomorrow, you could meet someone whose more intriguing than I am. Maybe a female architect with an eye for detail. Someone who shares a similar interest as you."

Ramsey dropped his fork on his plate and rubbed his mustache. "Do you hear the things you're saying to me?" he asked frowning. "No, I can't predict the future, but I don't need that ability to know that I want you. *You*, Gianna.

No one else." He blew a frustrated breath. "I wanted you to sign the papers because you wanted this. Because you trusted me. Because you know I could be a good man for you. That I'd take care of you."

"I know all those things, Ramsey, but I can't help but feel inadequate around you in every way. Even sitting here now, I feel like I don't belong."

"You belong because I want you here."

"And I hate to say this, I really do, but as I'm sitting here, I'm wondering how many women have sat in this very seat. How many women you've said these same words to. I don't know you all that well and—"

Ramsey pushed away from the table and walked out of the room.

Gianna closed her eyes and blew an even breath. She'd pissed him off. Was he coming back?

A few minutes later, Carson showed up. "Is he returning?"

Gianna glanced up at him. "I don't know. I think I made him angry."

"Are you going to finish up your dinner, Gianna?"

"No. I'm going to go to lie down for a while. I no longer have an appetite, Carson."

"Then I'll take care of clearing the table."

"I can help you."

"No. It's my job. I'm happy to do it," Carson said. "Oh, and by the way, I wasn't eavesdropping on your conversation but I can assure you, there hasn't been another woman sitting in that chair, or any of these chairs. You and your sister are the only women who've been here – well besides his mother, of course."

"Seriously?"

"Yes. I'm sure he was irritated about your assumption."

"Maybe I'll go talk to him."

"I would advise you to let him cool off for a bit. He has a bit of a temper."

"He does?"

"Yes."

"I've never seen it."

"He has subtle ways of taming it." Carson chuckled. "It's better than it used to be, but I hear it's a different story at the office."

"Well, thanks for the heads up, Carson. I guess I'll go to bed now."

Gianna got up to head in the direction of her guest bedroom, but she didn't want to. She wanted to seek Ramsey out and apologize since she had apparently offended him. But sometimes when people were frustrated and upset, they needed to work through it alone.

On the way to her room, she checked on Gemma briefly and then continued on to her room where she took a short shower and got into bed.

Chapter 19

BUSINESS HAD BEEN good all day at the bakery. Every time she turned around she was opening the oven door, pulling cupcakes out and putting some in. In the back of her mind, though, she knew she still had the situation with Ramsey to sort out. Maybe it wasn't a good idea to move in with a man she hardly knew. To sign papers agreeing to marry him. According to Carson, Ramsey had a temper and while she could tell he was one of those men who liked being in control of his life and business, she didn't think that would translate over to her.

She sighed heavily. That was the beautiful thing about being single. There was no one to answer to. No one to constantly strive to please. Being single meant you were free as a bird. You didn't have to answer a thousand questions before leaving your own house. With a man around, it was like cross-examination. She could see herself now, a year in with Ramsey, walking to the door with her purse, wearing a beautiful dress while he was on the couch with the remote watching football:

"Hey, where are you going?" he would ask.

And her response would be, "Out with Felicity. I'll be back in a lil' while, Ram."

"How long is a little while?"

She'd shrug. "Maybe three hours or so. We're doing appetizers and a movie."

"What movie?"

What does it matter? Dang! *"Not sure...something Felicity wanted to see."*

"And where are you eating appetizers?"

Blank stare

"Did you hear me?" he would ask.

"Probably somewhere by Northlake Mall."

"Do you have your phone?"

Why? So you can call and bug the crap out of me some more with your millions of questions?

"Gianna?"

"Yes, I have my phone."

Ugh...is this really how it would go down?

* * *

AS SHE BEGAN closing duties, she didn't know how to feel since Ramsey hadn't bothered calling her today nor had he stopped by. She walked to the front door, locked it and turned the *open* sign off. Then she answered her phone seeing that it was Felicity calling.

"Hey, Felicity," she drawled out.

"Goodness. You sound like you've been run over by a Mack diesel, and by Mack diesel, I mean Ramsey St. Claire." She cackled like the silly person she was.

Her strange tone of laughter made Gianna laugh, too, even when she didn't feel like laughing. "Whatever, girl. I'm tired of working this week for some reason."

"I know the reason, you little freak, you."

"What are you talking about?"

"Your boyfriend, or shall I say *husband* just left here a couple of hours ago."

"He did?"

"Affirmative...told me you were staying with him for the week. I was like, uh-uh, not my innocent, lil' Gianna, to which he laughed."

"Sorry. I forgot to tell you."

"How do you forget to tell your best friend something this monumental? And you sitting up here acting like you were so scared of him."

"I didn't say I was scared of him—"

Felicity changed her voice to mimic Gianna's when she said, "Oh, help me, Felicity. What am I going to do if he tries to kiss me? Oh...I'm such a damsel in distress."

"I'm going to choke you," Gianna said, amused.

"That's how you were acting."

"Okay, but then I realized he really liked me, so it wasn't so bad."

"Yeah. Okay."

"So, he really signed the papers?" Gianna asked.

"Yeah, he signed them. Why do you sound so surprised?"

"Because I pissed him off last night and haven't heard from him all day."

"Hmm...maybe that would explain why he

was so quiet and straight-faced," Felicity said. "He'd usually have something slick to say to me, just like Buick Regal."

Gianna giggled. "Stop calling him that before it sticks."

Felicity chuckled. "Anyway, so did Ramsey get those lips or what?"

"Felicity!"

"What? I have a right to know, don't I?"

"No."

"I beg to differ. I told you everything about my first kiss and first everything else."

"Yeah, when we were in *high school*. We're grown now. Some things you keep to yourself."

"Not this. Now, tell me. Did you kiss him?"

Gianna chewed on her lip. "Yes. We kissed."

Felicity screamed into the receiver, prompting Gianna to hold the phone away from her ear. "How was it? Did you see stars?"

Gianna blushed. "Did I see stars? Gosh, you watch way too many movies."

"Tell me. Did you?"

"Yes. I saw stars, constellations, planets, the moon's surface, discarded satellites floating around up there and galaxies that haven't been discovered yet. I saw it all."

Felicity screamed again and Gianna laughed. Then Gianna's body locked up when she felt arms encircling her from behind. She panicked a little because he – Ramsey – caught her off guard, but she knew the smell of her man. The feel of him. Before she could say a word, she felt his warm breath tickle her ear when he whispered, "Tell Felicity you'll call her back."

Right after he said it, he sucked her earlobe into his mouth.

Holding the phone, her hands steadily trembling, she said, "Fe-fe-fe-li-li—"

"I heard his voice," Felicity said. "And by all that stuttering, I take it you gotta go, huh?"

"Mmm hmm..." she managed to get out.

"Okay." Felicity giggled. "Bye, girl."

Gianna ended the call then turned around to look at Ramsey. He'd shaven she first noticed. Darn. The facial hair looked good on him, but she knew it wouldn't be long before it grew back. "You know I hate it when you sneak up on me."

"No, you don't," he said embracing her.

She smiled, hugging him back and allowing herself to feel his arms around her and smell him – his cologne. His skin. "I thought you were mad at me," she said.

"I *am* mad at you," he responded, dipping his head to take a small kiss from her lips. "Well, not mad." He took another kiss. "Frustrated." He took yet another. "I want so much from you in such a little amount of time, but no worries. I can wait. You don't leave me much choice in the matter."

"Ramsey, about what I said last night—"

"It's forgotten," he said, interrupting her apology.

"Ramsey, please just let me say it."

"Say what? I've forgiven you. There's nothing left to be said, Gianna."

"There is...that I'm sorry for making assumptions about you."

"And I forgive you, sweet lips."

She blushed, looking down, noticing for the first time, that he had on a suit. "Why are you dressed up?"

"I had to visit one of my sites today."

"A work site?"

"Yes."

"And you had to dress up for that?"

"I did. Anything relating to my business, I like to look professional."

Gianna nodded. He definitely looked professional. "So, that's why you didn't come to see me today?"

"You were looking for me, baby?"

"This morning, I was. I thought you were still mad."

"I had errands to run. Guess what else I did today."

"What's that?" she asked, staring up into his eyes.

"Made you mine. Felicity probably told you, but I went by Wedded Bliss to sign the papers, Mrs. St. Claire. Oh, how I like the sound of that."

Her stomach tightened. Felicity told her that Ramsey had stopped by to sign the papers, but actually hearing it from him made it real. She instantly felt hot like her body temperature had shot up a few degrees. It didn't help that she felt dizzy at the same time.

"Hey, you're not going to faint on me, are you?"

"N-n-no. I just need to sit down for a moment."

"Okay," Ramsey said holding her hand, leading her to the office. He helped her sit down then said, "I came by here to help you with your closing work. I'll take care of sweeping and mopping and cleaning the bathroom. You do whatever work you need to do on the computer, okay."

She nodded.

Ramsey pulled the door closed, hoping the time would help her get her bearings after he just told her he'd signed the papers. Did she think he wasn't going to sign? That he wasn't serious about the marriage? When everything in him wanted any and everything she had to offer?

He got up this morning with her on his mind. Granted, he had some work-related tasks to accomplish, but the day was all about her. He'd given Carson a massive grocery list – all items Gianna needed to make butter pecan cupcakes – a hundred of them. And he'd hired a chef for the night. Since signing the papers, he wanted the night to be special for her. Wanted her to know he was one-hundred percent committed to the marriage even though it was one formed by unconventional means. He even went to Zales and chose her ring. He'd spent an hour going back and forth between rings – large and small. Since she wasn't the loud, boisterous type, he knew she wouldn't like a large stone and he wasn't feeling the small one, so he settled on a medium-sized one. A white gold, two-carat certified diamond solitaire ring that he knew would look perfect on her finger.

And now he was here, mopping the floors after he was done cleaning the bathroom and sweeping. He took out the garbage and made sure the front door was locked. Then he slowly opened her office door.

Gianna glanced away from her computer screen to look at him. "Hey."

"I'm done," he told her. "Is there anything else I can do?"

"No. I was just checking inventory."

"Is there a problem?"

She shook her head. "No."

"Are you sure?"

"Yes."

"Well, are you ready to go, then?"

"Yes. Let me just close out here." Gianna logged out of the inventory system and said, "Okay. I'm ready."

He opened the door wider as she walked closer to him and then they headed out the back where she locked up the rear entrance.

"We'll let your car stay here," Ramsey said. "I want you to ride home with me."

"Hunh?" Gianna frowned.

"You've been working all day," he said. "I want you to ride with me."

"But I can't leave my car here overnight, Ramsey."

"Why can't you? What are they going to do? Tow it?"

"They might."

He smirked. "They're not going to tow your car, sweetness."

"But—"

"I want you to ride with me, Gianna. I realize it's a forty-five-minute drive, and I also realize it's a sacrifice you made in order to spend the week with me. This evening, I would like for you to ride with me," he said, staring at her lips.

"Okay," she caved, then as she walked around to the passenger side of his Range, he reached around her to open the door.

"Thanks, Ramsey."

"You're welcome."

He closed the door after she got in then walked around to the driver side. When he started down the highway, he glanced over at her. He wondered if she realized this was the first time they were ever alone in a car together. If she felt the waves of electricity running back and forth between them. He didn't doubt that she could. That's why she'd interlocked her hands and when that wasn't helping to calm her nerves, she'd switch to crossing her arms. And she was quiet. Uneasy. How could she be after they'd just kissed thirty minutes ago?

After driving for about fifteen minutes, intermittently watching her behave this way, he asked, "Gianna, are you okay?"

"Yes," she answered quickly, almost before he could get the whole question out.

"What are you thinking about? And don't shrug. Don't tell me you weren't thinking about anything. Be honest with me."

"I was thinking about you signing the papers. Thinking about being something I don't know how to be."

"My wife?" He glanced at her and then back to the road.

"Yes. Your wife."

"It's really nothing for you to worry about, but to ease your fears, we'll talk more about that over dinner."

"Okay."

Chapter 20

WHEN THEY PULLED up in the driveway, Gianna jumped out of the Range and jogged toward the front door. Since she knew the security code for the keypad lock, she let herself in.

Once inside, she ran upstairs, calling out Gemma's name.

"I'm in the dining room," she heard Gemma yell.

She turned around, jogged back downstairs and saw Gemma sitting at the dining room table with Carson.

"What are you doing?" she asked, nearly out of breath.

"We were just eating. Carson made a potato soup that was out of this world. He put some cheese and green onions—"

"Shallots," Carson interrupted her to say.

"Oh, right. Shallots," Gemma said. "I just think it's the boujee way to say onions."

Gianna smiled. "And you're feeling okay today, Gem?"

"Yes. I feel fine," Gemma said, feigning cheerfulness.

"Where's Harriet?" Gianna asked.

"I had her leave early since Carson was

cooking dinner for Gemma," Ramsey answered from behind her.

Gianna turned around and looked at him. She wanted to ask him something...um...right – why he didn't bother to tell her that Harriet was leaving early today, but just making eye contact with him nearly snatched her breath away. *I can't believe he's mine.*

"Gianna?"

She blinked, then focused on Ramsey.

"Yes?"

"Why don't you go get changed for dinner?"

"Oh. Right. Okay." She walked over to Gemma first, kissed her on the cheek and said, "I'm glad you're okay."

Gemma smiled.

* * *

AFTER GIANNA TOOK a quick shower, she put on a simple black maxi dress that was so long, it dragged the floor. Then she removed her hairnet, ran her fingers through her hair and shook it a little to give it some life, letting it fall around her shoulders. She added a bit of pink gloss to her lips, then with bare feet, she headed to the door to exit the bedroom. When she opened the door, she saw Carson standing there and threw her hand over her heart.

"Goodness, Carson. You scared me."

"Sorry about that, Mrs. St. Claire."

She beamed. He was calling her Mrs. St. Claire already? "Um...is Gemma okay?"

"Yes. Gemma is fine. I've come to take you to

dinner, madam."

"To...to take me to dinner? I know where the dining room is, Carson."

"I know you do, madam, but Ramsey has made different dinner arrangements for you tonight. Shall we?" Carson bent his arm so she could loop her arms with his.

After she accepted, he headed towards the set of stairs that led up to what Ramsey liked to call the penthouse suite – his bedroom – his entire third-floor oasis. "I'm having dinner in Ramsey's...in...in...his bedroom?"

Instead of answering her, Carson continued on upstairs, passing through Ramsey's bedroom door and on to through the double French doors and out onto the balcony where Gianna froze. There sat Ramsey at a table with white candles and champagne flutes. Strings of lights floated above their heads while at least ten dozen red roses decorated the immediate area. A bottle of champagne rested in a silver ice bucket.

Ramsey stood up. "Thank you, Carson."

"You're welcome, Sir," he said, then walked away.

Gianna didn't budge.

"Gianna?"

Her eyes rolled up to meet his, but her body didn't physically move an inch.

Ramsey walked over to her, took her hand into his and said, "Welcome to dinner."

"What is all of this, Ramsey?"

"It's dinner for you. For us. Today marks a special occasion for us. Wouldn't you agree?"

"Um...yes."

"Then, right this way, beautiful," he said, taking a few steps, then pulling a chair out for her.

Gianna was still in somewhat of a shock as she looked around, taking it all in. He did this for her? For them? To mark the beginning of their marriage? Wow.

As if she wasn't already blown away, a chef with the whole chef getup and all came strolling outside with a tray. He placed two salads on the table in front of the both of them.

When he walked away, Gianna looked up at Ramsey and asked, "Who is he?"

"A chef I use from time-to-time for special occasions."

"Oh."

"Try the salad. It's amazing."

She took a fork full to her mouth. *How could he make salad taste so scrumptious and when she made it, it tasted like grass?*

"Good?"

"Yes. Delicious." She dabbed her mouth with a napkin. "Ramsey, this is too much."

"What's too much?"

"This," she said looking around.

"Nothing is ever too much for you, Gianna."

She held his serious gaze for a moment, saw flames from the candles dance in his eyes and looked away.

"I realize that my presence can be intimidating for you. That everything I do for you is probably, in your mind, going above and beyond...doing too much, but I won't apologize for it. It's my job to see to it that you, my wife, have everything you need in life. Everything you want. Everything you desire. I recognize your uneasiness around me, Gianna, but I feel it's my duty to keep pushing the envelope so that one day, you can sit down to dinner with me without your hands trembling."

"I will never get to that point."

He smiled. She probably wouldn't but it would be fun getting her to try. "Do you want children?"

"Children?"

"Yes. Children. I brought up the subject last night, but you never answered me."

"Um...I think so."

He raised a brow. "You think? That's something women are pretty definite about."

"I know. It's just that I haven't had much time to think about what I want in life because of—"

"Gemma. I get it. Now, I'm asking you what you want."

Gianna opened her mouth to speak but then thought about what she would say in more detail before she actually said it.

"Let me be more specific," Ramsey said, "Can you see yourself being the mother of my children?"

Gianna frowned.

"Can you?"

She nodded. "Yes."

Ramsey smiled, satisfied with her answer.

Out of nowhere, she said, "We're complete opposites."

"I realize that."

"Is that what initially attracted you to me?"

"No. I told you what initially attracted me to you."

"Yes, the heart thing, but—"

"No buts. That was it."

"Being that we're opposites, Ramsey, you don't foresee that being a compatibility issue?"

"No. I don't."

"How can you not?"

"Give me a scenario where it would be a problem."

"Um..." Gianna chewed on her bottom lip.

He looked at her as she did so. Everything in him wanted to jump across the table and suck that lip into his mouth.

"You don't think that would be an issue?"

"Huh?" he asked. Had she said something?

"You didn't hear what I just said?" she asked him.

"No. I was so busy daydreaming about how I wanted to suck your bottom lip into my mouth."

Gianna's face flushed.

The chef came outside on the balcony with two plates of spaghetti.

Gianna smiled, recognizing they were having a similar dinner to the meal she'd ordered on their first date at Luce. Before the chef walked away, he popped the top off of the bottle of champagne, poured some in their flutes and headed back inside.

"See, that's a prime example of what I'm talking about," Gianna said. "I couldn't just blurt out how I was daydreaming about sucking your lips, but you tell me stuff like that and it's not a problem."

"Okay, run the scenario by me again."

"Alright. Let's say you wanted to do something outrageous that I would be opposed to. Like skydiving, for instance."

Ramsey chuckled. "Regal told you about the skydiving, huh?"

"He did. My question is, would you be upset with me if I didn't want to do it?"

"No, and I would never force you to do something you didn't want to do. I'd just use my power of persuasion to coax you into doing things."

Gianna playfully narrowed her eyes at him. "Goodness. You're going to be so much trouble."

"You're just now realizing that, sweetheart?"

She giggled.

"On a more serious note, I only have another week off of work."

"Okay."

"I want to be there with you for Gemma's consultation and Carson has already booked a suite for us. We'll fly out Tuesday morning. The consultation is Wednesday."

Gianna didn't say anything. But her chewing slowed as she thought about how much he was willing to invest in this relationship for her sake.

"Talk to me," he said when he could tell she'd been busy cramming thoughts in her mind.

"I was just thinking about how much you're doing for me. I could never repay you, Ramsey."

"Gianna, I haven't felt this much excitement, this much longing, this much of anything in my heart for a long time. You've already repaid me, baby. Now, I want to know how you'd feel about me going back to work in a week's time."

"I think you will need to and it will be good because I'm at work during the day anyway and—"

"That's another thing. I don't want you working long hours anymore."

Gianna grimaced. "It's my job, Ramsey."

"I realize that. I also realize you get there around seven in the morning and you don't leave until around seven in the evening. I don't like that."

"But—"

"No buts. It's too much for you."

She frowned. "Are you serious?"

"Yes. I am. What's makes you think I'm not?"

"Don't know. I just didn't expect you to be controlling."

"Controlling? I'm trying to look out for your well being and you call that controlling?"

"Yes. You can be my husband, fine, but you don't have to tell me how to live and run my own business."

Ramsey lowered his fork to his plate of half-eaten spaghetti. "I'm not telling you how to live, Gianna."

"That's what it feels like."

"Of course it would feel that way to you because you don't know how it feels to be taken care of. You don't know how to accept my generosity. I get it. You've worked your whole life, through blood, sweat and tears, taking care of your sister when that is not your responsibility, by the way, but you do it because you love her. I admire that in you. I also hate that everything—all of this responsibility—fell on your back. And you've been doing this for how long? Since you were a teenager? You were forced to be your sister's mother while you were still a teenager. And you've been going nonstop ever since. I hate that you get up every morning, even on Saturday and work your butt off at the bakery. I hate that your parents left you with their responsibilities. Hate the fact that you go to bed some nights crying yourself to sleep because you don't know what's going to happen from one day to the next. Don't know how your bills are going to get paid. I hate that for you, Gianna. That's why I step in as forceful as I do because I realize I need to work quickly to take these stresses away from you because there's only so much a person can handle and you, my sweet wife, can't handle much more."

Gianna felt the blood drain from her face while her eyes filled with tears. "That's why I don't like you working so much. It's not about me being controlling. Look at me," he told her the moment she looked way from him. When she connected her misty eyes to his again, he said, "It's not about me being controlling. It's about me stepping in and doing my job as your husband to make sure you have everything you need. I *am* your husband now. *I* take care of *you* now, Gianna, and I take my responsibility very seriously. You've never had that—somebody taking care of you—but you do now and maybe it's going to take a while for you to realize the difference in a controlling person and one who wants to take care of you, but I will say this. I won't put you in a cage, tell you where to go. What to wear, where to eat. I'm just trying to be here for you. To be present for you. To take the stress away from you and be a man for you. Your rock. Your protector. Your everything. Tell me you see that."

Gianna's blinked the tears away from her eyes. Clearing her throat, she spoke clearly and softly when she said, "Yes. I see that, Ramsey. It's just that, like you said, all my life, it's just been me."

"Well, now, it's you and me. Okay?"

She nodded.

Ramsey stood up. "With that being said," he took a step closer to kneel down in front of her. "I want to make our engagement and marriage official."

Gianna swallowed the lump in her throat. It was one thing to know that they were married on paper, but a completely different thing altogether to have him holding her left hand, staring into her eyes, on bended knee making it all *official*. "Ramsey...wha-what are you doing?"

He watched a tear roll down her face and

closed his eyes, forcing himself to take it. "The more you get to know me, the more you'll realize that I'm in no way perfect. I have many flaws—ones that I'm sure will present themselves to you at some point during our marriage. But the one thing—the only thing you need to know about me is that I'm loyal. I will always be loyal to you and I hope that on this journey, we get to know more and more about each other every single day. And I will do everything that is within my power to make sure you're happy. Your days of struggling are over. Your days of crying yourself to sleep at night—over."

Ramsey used his thumbs to wipe the tears from her face. "Gianna, you've already married me so I'll ask you this—will you keep an open mind, go on this journey with me, let me be there for you, comfort you, protect you and be a husband to you?"

"Yes," she answered with trembling lips.

Ramsey slid the ring onto her trembling finger. And then he slid his tongue between her trembling lips, tasting spaghetti sauce on her tongue. Still in the kneeling position, he pulled her closer to him until he felt her legs around him and stood straight up, taking her to the chaise lounge chair where he lowered her, then eased on top of her until her back made contact with the cushion. And then he lowered himself on top of her until his body blanketed hers beneath the night sky, beneath the romantic lights and clamped his lips down on hers.

This kiss was different from the others

they'd shared. This kiss was the first time he was kissing her as *his*. The kiss he'd been holding back all day long and now was relieving the pressure that had been building at his gut with wanting to connect his mouth to hers. He angled his mouth, going deeper, wanting to kiss her into understanding. Wanting her to know that she was his woman.

Gianna whimpered, her hands settling at the nape of his neck allowing him to have full control. Goodness. He was so dominant and she was well aware of him being there, his body comfortably on top of her while his tongue bathed the inside of her mouth as if manually searching for her heart. And she was feeling more sensations course through her body. She'd never desired a man before Ramsey and she knew she would never desire one after. He'd awakened the deepest desires inside of her and a part of it scared her. Where did this passion come from so suddenly?

A better question was, how could she make it stop? She wasn't ready for this. She didn't know the first thing about passion. What did a woman who practiced kissing on a Fuji apple know about passion and desires? She could hang with him with the kissing – well a little – but then his lips, his mouth locked onto her neck like a leech and her body jerked so hard it lifted up from the cushion. Still, he didn't let up.

"Ramsey," she whispered. Panting. "Ramsey."

"Huh?" he said.

She assumed he made the *huh* sound so he didn't have to take his mouth off of her.

"What are you—? Oh, goodness." Breathing heavily, she started again, "What are you doing to my neck?"

"Sucking it. Licking it. Rolling my tongue in circles on it. Marking my territory."

"You're giving me convulsions."

"I know. I like feeling your body convulse beneath mine." He took a single kiss from her lips then rotated his body so that he was lying next to her. He pulled her into his arms. "Don't worry, Gianna. I want to take things slow with you." He brushed a kiss across her temple, then buried a hand in her hair, lowering his head to smell her strands. "Your hair smells like your bakery. Ahh...smells so good." He noticed it before but never said anything.

She giggled. "I know. It's a business flaw."

"It's not a flaw. I love the fact that you smell so sweet. Makes me want to gobble you up."

She smiled.

He found her hand and interlocked their fingers. "Gianna, I meant what I said about your work hours. I think we should cut your closing time back to five. Additionally, I want to hire someone to help you out."

"I have no idea where to begin with hiring someone."

"If it's okay with you, I'll put an ad in the paper and we could have some interviews," Ramsey said.

"We?"

"Yes. I wouldn't leave you to do it all alone."

"But you're going back to work soon."

"Right, about that," he said, adjusting his position on the chair so he had a full view of her face. "I've been thinking about taking another month off."

"Please don't say it's because of me," she said.

"It's because of you," he said, then took a kiss from her lips.

"Ramsey, I don't want you to change your life for me."

"It's too late for that, don't you think?"

"But—"

He placed his index finger on her lips. "I told you...there's nothing I won't do for you."

She gripped his wrist and pulled his hand away from her mouth. "But, Ramsey—"

"I have a home office. I have full access to everything I have access to at work, and I have my brothers. I'll be fine."

"Are you sure?"

"Yes. I want to be with you. You're my priority now, Gianna."

She smiled, then went quiet, thinking about how good it felt to be someone's priority.

"Talk to me," he whispered.

"About what?"

"I can always tell when you're holding something back from me."

"I was just thinking about how grateful I am to have you in my life. I've never had anyone do anything for me. Well, except Felicity."

"Well, now you have me, Cupcake." He kissed her again. "Will you spend the night with me?"

"In your bed?"

He grinned. "Yes. In my bed."

"No!"

Ramsey laughed. "Okay, when I say spend the night with me, it has nothing to do with me touching your *cupcake*. I promise. I just want to hold you in my arms. In my bed."

She glanced at his eyes. His mouth. Both were equally seductive.

"I promise," he said, still smiling.

"That wicked dimple in the corner of your cheek is not convincing me."

He chuckled. Dang, she was a hard bargain and he loved it. A woman saying *no* to him was a rarity, and he actually enjoyed the challenge. "Okay," he said clearing his throat. "I mean it, sweetness. I won't touch you unless you want me to."

"Um...no. I can't. It's too much, too soon. I hope you understand."

"Oh, baby, you're killing me."

"I don't want it to be weird," she said. "I've never shared a bed with a man before and even though I trust that you won't touch me, I'm just not ready yet."

"Okay. I respect that, but you better believe I'm going to make up for it somehow."

"I'm sure you will."

Chapter 21

Gianna was ready to leave for the bakery at six in the morning when she remembered Ramsey had driven her home yesterday evening. She'd left her car at the bakery per his request. What was she going to do now? Take his car? Was he even up this early in the morning?

When she turned away from the front door to go seek him out – boom – there he was standing on the bottom step staring at her. He had on a pair of flimsy black mesh gym shorts and he wasn't wearing a shirt. *Mercy.* Her eyes widened to take in the full scope of him. Of pure, male gorgeousness. His abs were so toned, his six pack looked like a set of grenades. His chest was beefy and thick. And then his shoulders were well-defined and very linebacker*ish*. And those shorts...goodness. They just hung right around his waist. They were loose enough to where she could see why they were comfortable for workouts but clingy enough to put his manliness on full display. Things she couldn't see when he was in his normal clothes she could see clearly now. He had the body of an Adonis. And he had it on full display. What was he trying to do? Give her heart palpitations first thing in the morning? As it was, she wasn't a morning person. He knew that. And this morning, she needed to get going but *somebody* convinced her to leave her car at the bakery.

She frowned, dug deep to find her voice and asked, "Just what do you think you're doing walking around here with your tits out?"

Ramsey looked down at his chest, then back up at her and cracked a smile. "They're called pectorals, baby. You wanna touch? Get acquainted with them?"

Her eyes narrowed. "No. I want to go to work. How am I supposed to get to work today?"

"You're not going to work today."

"Oh, yes I am," she said, crossing her arms.

He smiled. "You really are a different person in the morning. I feel like I'm married to two women. On one end, I have the nice, shy, sweet Gianna who has this major crush on me and then there's evil, *rah-rah*, morning Gianna who looks at me with dark brown eyes like she's ready to choke me."

"I *am* ready to choke you. I need to get to work, Ramsey."

"I told you, you're not going to work today."

"Um, did you forget I have to bake a million freakin' cupcakes for Jennifer, your secretary?"

"Her name's Judy."

"Judy, Jennifer...whoever she is—she ordered ninety-eight cupcakes for today."

"Ninety-six," he corrected. "And *Judy* will get them," Ramsey said, taking the last step

260

down to walk up to her. He manually uncrossed her arms and took her left hand into his right as he headed towards the kitchen.

"We're heading in the wrong direction. I need to go towards the front door, not back here."

"You need to trust your man."

"My man needs to give me the keys to his car?"

"No, your man does not. I mean, I would, but you don't need my car. You know why, sweetness?"

"Ramsey, I don't have time for this little back and forth with you."

"We're making cupcakes here now stop panicking."

"Here? Are you kidding? We can't make cupcakes here. You don't have—" Gianna looked at the island when they stepped into the kitchen noticing it was full of ingredients. Butter, cream, milk, vanilla extract, powdered sugar, pecans, brown sugar, all purpose flour, shortening, granulated sugar, buttermilk, eggs, baking soda and a slew of other items that she probably would or wouldn't need. And then she saw what looked to be a brand new, teal mixer – two of them – and cupcake baking pans, liners and two white aprons.

"Ramsey, what did you do?"

"I sent Carson shopping to get everything we needed to make over a hundred cupcakes."

"Why?"

"Because I didn't want you working at the bakery today and I knew you wanted to fulfill this order, so let's get busy. And, just for clarification, by *get busy*, I mean let's start making and baking some cupcakes."

"You're a sneaky somebody. You planned this."

"Yeah, I did," Ramsey said, tying on an apron over his six pack. "Suit up, sugar lips."

Gianna grinned, even when she didn't feel like it. This isn't where she was supposed to bake. She baked in *her* bakery. The Boardwalk Bakery. Not Ramsey St. Claire's gourmet kitchen. But cupcakes had to be made, and she didn't have time to pout when the people of St. Claire Architects would be waiting for cupcakes. She lowered her purse in one of the barstools then removed a hairnet from it, placing it over her hair. She'd already had it in a bun, the same way she did her hair whenever she had to work.

Heading over to the sink, she washed her hands, then stared at the island full of stuff.

"I'll be your assistant today."

Gianna hid a smirk. He looked good wearing an apron over his bare chest, but boy was he sexy. Looked like he could pose for a bakery calendar with a name like *Hot Men Who Bake* or *Baking Me Crazy*.

She chuckled as she reached for a large mixing bowl. "Do you remember how to make to the batter?"

"I know I need some flour," he said, opening the bag.

"Yep, and baking soda. Mix that up first."

"Yes, ma'am," he said, looking at her. He

liked how serious she was about her work – loved that she wanted it done right. He was the same way when it came to his design work. Every detail had to be perfect or he'd scrap the whole thing. Start over.

While he worked on that, she mixed butter, granulated sugar, adding egg yolk and vanilla extract. Then she instructed him to add some of his flour mixture.

"About how many will this make?" he asked.

"Probably three dozen. And we need a total of eight."

"Cool, so we'll have to do this all over again?"

"Yes, but I think I'll have you start on the frosting."

"Okay. Tell me what I need to do, baby."

She smiled, trying to get accustomed to his terms of endearment. She was his baby. She'd never been anyone's baby. "Okay, it's really simple. Just get that bowl," she said, pointing to the clear one. "And you'll need the cream cheese, butter, confectioners' sugar and vanilla extract."

"That's it?"

"Yes. Blend the butter and the cream cheese really well, then add the sugar and vanilla extract. Once everything is at a creamy consistency, you can cover it and put it in the refrigerator."

He grinned. "You like telling me what to do, don't you?"

"How else are you supposed to know how to make cream cheese frosting?" she asked.

"Right. Let me get to work before I get fired."

Gianna grinned and shook her head. She placed cupcake liners in three pans and filled them, putting all three in the oven. Then she started making another mixture for the second round.

Working quickly, she filled another three pans and then prepared the last batch. It was enough to fill three more pans. Even though she only needed two more, she liked making extras just for backup.

She glanced at her watch. She wondered if Ramsey told Judy to come to his house to pick up the cupcakes. She wanted to ask, but he was seriously concentrating on making the frosting, mixing and blending so well, she could see the muscle in his arm flex and move while he worked. He was beating the crap out of that frosting and she loved his commitment to the project. "Ramsey."

He looked to his right to see the smile on her face.

"Yes?"

She chuckled. "If you beat that cream cheese frosting any more, you're going to jail for assault and battery."

His beautiful smile showed. "Why are you intent on sending me to jail? First you accused me of breaking into your house, and now you got me for assault and battery. On some cream cheese frosting."

Gianna laughed harder. "Sorry. It was kinda funny, but I admire your dedication."

"Just keep in mind that I'm this dedicated to everything I do. I don't want it to come as a surprise to you later."

"Then I appreciate the warning."

"You're welcome, sweetness. Now, I want you to taste this to see if I did it to your specifications." He took a spoonful of the frosting and while holding the spoon in his left hand, he dipped the index finger of his right hand in the frosting and then held his finger in front of her mouth.

She was already laughing when she said, "Ain't no way I'm licking your finger."

"Go on," he said, then chewed at his bottom lip. "I licked yours. It's about time you got your revenge on mine."

Giggling, she said, "Trust me, I don't need revenge. Give me the spoon."

"Nope. I want you to taste my finger. I mean the cream cheese." He chuckled. "Go on, Gianna. What is there to be shy about? Huh? I've had your tongue in my mouth before. You've had my tongue in your mouth, and now you don't want to lick my finger?"

Gianna nervously considered his request. He was right. What was there to be nervous about? If she could handle his tongue, why not his finger? "Okay, okay." She opened her mouth and leaned toward his finger but instead of putting his finger inside, he spread frosting on her lips. Before she could protest, he leaned forward and pressed his lips to hers, sucking frosting from her lips, the sensation causing his mouth to water for more. He lifted her up off of the floor and found a clear section on the island where he placed her, crawled on top of her and made the island their bed as he delved deeper inside of her mouth, kissing the sweetness right off of her.

Gianna moaned as her hands touched the back of his head, pulling him in to her, fully giving in to his seductive cream cheese kiss. And she thought about what a chocolate kiss would taste like. A lemon kiss. The possibilities were endless. Right now, though, she needed to focus on *this* kiss because he certainly was. Several times, she'd felt his tongue at the back of her mouth. What? Did he want her to swallow him? Jeez. He loved to kiss deeply and she just tried her best to hang on. To breathe. To...

"What in the *world* is happening here?" Romulus asked as he stepped into the kitchen with Royal, Regal, Gemma and Carson.

"I don't know," Royal said. "Looks like some weird cupcake orgy."

Gemma chuckled. Carson had introduced her to Ramsey's brothers immediately after he'd let them in a few minutes ago.

"They were supposed to be in here making cupcakes," Gemma said. "Instead, they're making little cupcake babies."

Carson grinned. He'd never seen this side of Ramsey. Gianna brought out a different side of him.

"*That's* the sweet, innocent cupcake girl?" Royal asked, laughing.

"Yes. My sister is sweet and innocent. It's

your brother bringing out this side of her."

"The freaky side," Romulus said.

Royal chuckled.

"Yo, Ram, can you come up for air?" Regal asked.

Unfazed by their presence, Ramsey kept on kissing Gianna but he could feel her uneasiness with knowing they had an audience. He didn't care about an audience, but since she did, he suctioned his mouth away from hers, smiled at her and then looked up at his brothers and Gemma and said, "Hey, I'm not done here just yet. Carson has breakfast ready. Wait for us in the dining room. I gotta get me some more of this," he said, dipping his head to a giggly Gianna yet again. "What are you laughing for, girl?"

"You're too much," she said.

He hovered over her.

"How are you going to kiss me like that in front of your brothers? I'm so embarrassed."

"Why? You're mine. I'm yours. This is our house. I'll kiss you wherever I want to kiss you."

"I don't want their first impression of me being an image of me swallowing your tongue."

He smiled wickedly. "See, this is what you get for not spending the night with me last night."

"Oh, is that what it is?"

"Yes. I couldn't do this last night, couldn't sleep for wanting to taste your lips, so the only way I could get to sleep was to think about fulfilling one of my fantasies when we got up in the morning."

"Fantasies?"

"Yes. Kissing frosting off of your lips." He eased off of her then when he was standing on the floor again, he helped her down. "Let me run upstairs and get dressed so we can eat some breakfast with my brothers."

"And why didn't you tell me they were coming over?"

With a sneaky grin, he said, "It slipped my mind."

"Nothing slips that sharp mind of yours."

When they reached the second floor, he said, "I didn't tell you because I didn't want you to panic. Meeting my brothers shouldn't cause you any trepidation."

"I didn't even see their faces since you had me pinned to the island."

Ramsey smirked. "You didn't miss anything. They're all ugly."

"Now, I know that's a lie. Regal could be your twin and you're so handsome, sometimes I can't stand it."

"Keep talking like that and they won't see us for breakfast. It ain't nothing for me to run back to the kitchen, grab the rest of that frosting and really get things poppin'."

Backing away from him, Gianna said, "Go get dressed, Ramsey. I'll meet you downstairs."

He chuckled. "Okay, Mrs. St. Claire."

Gosh, he knew how to make her blush, and she did so until she was in her guest bedroom. For the first time in her life, she was experiencing a level of happiness that only he'd been able to provide and that brought a smile to her face. She walked to the bathroom, pulled the hairnet from her head but left her hair in a bun. She wiped leftover buttercream from her face and the light trail of it that Ramsey had licked to her neck. Her body shivered at the way he'd done so. He was already proving to be more than she could handle.

* * *

"REGAL, YOU'VE ALREADY met Gianna," Ramsey said as he stepped into the dining room with Gianna's hand in his.

"Yes, and I just met Gemma," Regal said.

Ramsey squeezed Gianna's hand. "Okay, so Gianna, this is my brother Romulus."

"Nice to meet you, Gianna," Romulus said, lifting his hand in a single wave.

"Nice to meet you, too, Romulus," she replied.

"And the troublemaker, I mean troubleshooter sitting next to Gemma is Royal," Ramsey told her.

"Nice to meet you, Gianna. Glad to see you survived that encounter with the wilder beast this morning," Royal quipped.

Gianna was mortified, watching the smile form on the brother's faces while her cheeks turned red. After looking at them all together, she could see the similarities in their appearances now. You could look at them and tell they were related. They all had those same black eyes. Similar builds. Romulus and Royal were a shade lighter in complexion as Ramsey had told her during one of their earlier conversations.

Ramsey pulled out a chair for Gianna to sit. Then he sat next to her. Royal was to her right. And Gemma sat next to Royal. Regal and Romulus were on the opposite side of the table.

Ramsey spoke up and said, "In case you were wondering why they're here, Gianna, I asked my brothers to come over for a status meeting. They're going to take the cupcakes back to SCA when the meeting is over. First, though, we'll eat breakfast."

"Okay," Gianna said, glancing around the table at the brothers again.

"Alright. Let's dig in," Ramsey said. "We have a lot to cover and a lot of cupcakes to frost afterward."

He looked at Gianna and left a kiss on her cheek, then handed her a basket of biscuits.

Gianna took one and passed them to Royal.

Royal took one and was handing them to Gemma, but her eyes were going closed like she was falling asleep. He leaned closer to her and said, "Hey, sleepyhead, do you want a biscuit?"

Gemma eyes opened when she heard his voice so close to her ear. She looked at Royal and said groggily, "Oh, yes. Thank you." Taking the basket from him, her hand touched his and he frowned.

"Are you always this hot?" he asked her quietly so the rest of the table didn't hear him. He knew her story, knew she had cancer and that Ramsey and Gianna were trying to help her get better.

Gemma grinned lazily. "I appreciate you trying to be nice, but I walk around with a scarf tied around my head because I'm losing hair from one dose of chemo that didn't work. There's nothing *hot* about me."

"I'm talking about your temperature, Gemma," Royal said scooting closer to her.

"Right. Of course you are." Because why would a hot guy like you think I'm hot?

He placed his palm on her forehead and said, "You're burning up. I'm not a doctor but I know when someone has an elevated temperature."

"I'm fine," she said. "Will you stop?"

"What's going on?" Gianna said leaning forward to get a good view of Royal and Gemma.

"Your sister has a temperature?" Royal said.

Gemma glanced up and saw all eyes were on her now. Irritated, she said, "My God, will everyone just eat?"

Gianna stood up and walked over to her sister. She looked at her. Her eyes were bloodshot red, filling with tears. "Gem, you *are* burning up. We're going to have to get you to a doctor."

"No, I just need to lie down," Gemma said attempting to stand up, feeling weak. Dizzy.

Royal stood up, too, wanting to assist her in the event she needed help.

Ramsey rose to his feet as well.

"Gem," Gianna said, holding her arm, "I have to take you to the doctor. You shouldn't have a fever this high. I can feel the heat radiating from your body."

"I just...I just wanna go to sleep," Gemma said before her eyes closed and she began falling face forward but Royal caught her.

"Gemma!" Gianna screamed.

"Carson, call 911," Ramsey instructed. "Royal, let's get her on the couch. Rom, bring some wet towels. We need to get her temperature down, asap."

"Yes, she has a pulse and she's breathing," Carson said to the operator. "But she sort of fainted, and she looks like she's out of it. Her eyes are closed and she's not moving, not making any sounds..."

Gianna kneeled next to her sister, holding her hot hand, in tears. "Gemma, please don't leave me. Please, please, please," she cried.

Ramsey wrapped his arms around Gianna. "She'll be okay. We'll make sure of it. The ambulance is on its way, sweetheart."

Regal ran to the front door, on lookout for the ambulance.

Romulus brought in the wet towels.

Royal took a towel and placed it on Gemma's forehead. Then he draped one around her face. Her neck. He checked her pulse. It was there, but weak. "How long for the ambulance, Carson?"

"It's a few minutes out," Carson responded, relaying what the 911 operator told him.

Royal readjusted the towels, flipping them to the cool side and lowering them on her forehead and neck again.

"I hear the ambulance," Regal said, still standing at the front door.

"They're almost here, Gemma," Gianna said, sobbing. "They're almost here, sweet girl."

And Ramsey squeezed her harder, trying his best to soak her pain into his heart in hopes of taking it away from her although he knew that wasn't possible. Still, it wouldn't stop him from trying. "It's going to be okay, Gianna?" he said softly. "Help is on the way, baby. It's going to be okay." He needed everything to be okay, because losing Gemma would break Gianna's heart, just like losing Leandra had broken his all those years ago and left it broken. He couldn't bear the thought of Gianna having that same overwhelming, traumatic heartbreak. The same loss.

* ~ *

Gemma was on the verge of visiting the cancer treatment center when she fell ill. What next? Is it too late to save her life? How will these new developments affect Ramsey and Gianna's new relationship? Find out in the final last installment, Baked With Love 3, coming soon.

Also by Tina Martin:

The Blackstone Family Series
*All books in this series are standalone novels and are full, complete stories. Read them in any order.

Evenings With Bryson
Leaving Barringer
Forever Us: Barringer and Calista Blackstone (A short story follow-up to *Leaving Barringer*. You must read *Leaving Barringer* before reading this short story)
The Things Everson Lost

A Lennox in Love Series
*All books in this series are standalone novellas and are full, complete stories. Read them in any order.

Claiming You
Making You My Business
Wishing That I Was Yours
Caught in the Storm with a Lennox (A Short Story Prequel to Claiming You)

Mine By Default Mini-Series:
*This is a continuation series that must be read in order.

Been In Love With You, Book 1
When Hearts Cry, Book 2
You Belong To Me, Book 3
When I Call You Mine, Book 4
Who Do You Love?, Book 5
Forever Mine, Book 6

The Champion Brothers Series:
*All books in this series are standalone novels and are full, complete stories. Read them in any order.

His Paradise Wife
When A Champion Wants You
The Best Thing He Never Knew He Needed
Wives And Champions
The Way Champions Love

The Accidental Series:
*This is a continuation series that must be read in order.

Accidental Deception, Book 1
Accidental Heartbreak, Book 2
Accidental Lovers, Book 3
What Donovan Wants, Book 4

Dying To Love Her Series:
*This is a continuation series that must be read in order.

Dying To Love Her
Dying To Love Her 2
Dying To Love Her 3

The Alexander Series:
*Books 1-5 must be read in order. Book 6 and the spinoff book, Different Tastes, can be read in any order as a standalone.

The Millionaire's Arranged Marriage, Book 1
Watch Me Take Your Girl, Book 2
Her Premarital Ex, Book 3
The Object of His Obsession, Book 4
Dilvan's Redemption, Book 5
His Charity Challenge, Book 6 (Heshan Alexander and Charity Eason)
Different Tastes (An Alexander Spin-off novel. Tamera Alexander's Story)

Non-Series Titles:
*Individual standalone books that are not part of a series.
Secrets On Lake Drive
Can't Just Be His Friend
All Falls Down
Just Like New to the Next Man
Falling Again
Vacation Interrupted
The Crush
Wasn't Supposed To Love Her
What Wifey Wants

ABOUT THE AUTHOR

TINA MARTIN is the author of forty-six romance titles and has been writing full-time since 2013. Readers praise Tina for her strong heroes, sweet heroines and beautifully crafted stories. When she's not writing, Tina enjoys watching movies, traveling, cooking and spending time with her family. She currently resides, in Charlotte, North Carolina with her husband and two young children.

You can email Tina at tinamartinbooks@gmail.com or visit her website for more information at www.tinamartin.net.

Made in the USA
Lexington, KY
04 November 2017